Great Expectations

孤星血淚

Original Author   Charles Dickens
Adaptors   Louise Benette, David Hwang
Illustrator   Helene Zarubina

WORDS
1000

MP3

Let's Enjoy Masterpieces!

All the beautiful fairy tales and masterpieces that you have encountered during your childhood remain as warm memories in your adulthood. This time, let's indulge in the world of masterpieces through English. You can enjoy the depth and beauty of original works, which you can't enjoy through Chinese translations.

The stories are easy for you to understand because of your familiarity with them. When you enjoy reading, your ability to understand English will also rapidly improve.

This series of **Let's Enjoy Masterpieces** is a special reading comprehension booster program, devised to improve reading comprehension for beginners whose command of English is not satisfactory, or who are elementary, middle, and high school students. With this program, you can enjoy reading masterpieces in English with fun and efficiency.

This carefully planned program is composed of 5 levels, from the beginner level of 350 words to the intermediate and advanced levels of 1,000 words. With this program's level-by-level system, you are able to read famous texts in English and to savor the true pleasure of the world's language.

The program is well conceived, composed of reader-friendly explanations of English expressions and grammar, quizzes to help the student learn vocabulary and understand the meaning of the texts, and fabulous illustrations that adorn every page. In addition, with our "Guide to Listening," not only is reading comprehension enhanced but also listening comprehension skills are highlighted.

In the audio recording of the book, texts are vividly read by professional American actors. The texts are rewritten, according to the levels of the readers by an expert editorial staff of native speakers, on the basis of standard American English with the ministry of education recommended vocabulary. Therefore, it will be of great help even for all the students that want to learn English.

Please indulge yourself in the fun of reading and listening to English through **Let's Enjoy Masterpieces**.

查爾斯·狄更斯

Charles Dickens
(1812–1870)

Charles Dickens is considered to be one of the greatest English novelists of the Victorian period. His works are characterized by attacks on social evils, injustice, and hypocrisy.

Charles Dickens was born in Landport on 7 February 1812. He couldn't receive an appropriate school education in his childhood because he was born to a poor family. He began to work at the age of 12 in a factory where he was paid six shillings a week.

In the early19th century, British capitalism began to flourish, bringing prosperity to the big cities in England. However, there were also dark sides to capitalism. Child labor thrived, and the working class suffered from great poverty. With an insight born from his own bitter experiences with social injustice, Charles Dickens began to write short stories in order to educate himself and was determined to achieve his quest for self-education and pull himself out of poverty.

His best-known works include *Great Expectations* and *Oliver Twist*. Dickens' novels are highly respected for vivid descriptions of the daily life of working-class people. He knew from his own experience their joys and sorrows. Dickens' brave and humorous portrayals also examine injustice and social contradictions.

He was often criticized for trying to appeal to the sentimental and melodramatic tastes of his readers. But the reason Dickens, along with Shakespeare, is held in high regard as a great English novelist is that he created characters full of humanity and

humor. These characters exhibit the faults, resilience, and vitality of real human beings.

On June 9, 1870, Charles Dickens died. His death was mourned by the entire world, and he was laid to rest in Westminster Abbey, alongside England's other great writers.

Great Expectations is considered by many critics to be Dickens' finest novel because of its tightly structured plot. The story is about a low-born young man, Pip, who rises out of a rough, deprived childhood. His desire for improvement in his social status takes him to a city, where he becomes a gentleman after a lawyer appears one day with the news that he inherited a large fortune.

However, social advancement and wealth become superficial standards of value that Pip learns to look beyond. He finds that it is not Miss Havisham, an eccentric old woman, who he assumed to be his secret benefactor, but Magwitch, an escaped convict whom he once helped briefly.

Also he discovers that Estella, Miss Magwitch's charge, who he has been in love with and imagines belonging to the upper class, is actually the daughter of the convict. Estella has been taught by Miss Havisham to break men's hearts as restitution for Miss Havisham's having been abandoned in the past.

The negative examples of Miss Havisham, a bitter woman who lives a life of hatred, and the coarse and cruel Bentley Drummle, who becomes Estella's husband, help Pip to see the absence of humanity hidden behind the fantasies of high-class life.

After many years of wandering, Pip finally returns home. He realizes the true inner worth of human beings and the ideals of a gentleman, through the examples of Magwitch, the convict, and Joe, Pip's poor uncle. Pip achieves this realization when he is able to understand that the care shown to him by the convict, whom he despised, and the sincere love of the village blacksmith Joe are truly great expectations.

HOW TO USE THIS BOOK
本書使用說明

① Original English texts

It is easy to understand the meaning of the text, because the text is rewritten according to the levels of the readers.

② Explanation of the vocabulary

The words and expressions that include vocabulary above the elementary level are clearly defined.

③ Response notes

Spaces are included in the book so you can take notes about what you don't understand or what you want to remember.

⌒ *Audio Recording*

In the audio recording, native speakers narrate the texts in standard American English. By combining the written words and the audio recording, you can listen to English with great ease.

Audio books have been popular in Britain and America for many decades. They allow the listener to experience the proper word pronunciation and sentence intonation that add important meaning and drama to spoken English. Students will benefit from listening to the recording twenty or more times.

After you are familiar with the text and recording, listen once more with your eyes closed to check your listening comprehension. Finally, after you can listen with your eyes closed and understand every word and every sentence, you are then ready to mimic the native speaker.

Then you should make a recording by reading the text yourself. Then play both recordings to compare your oral skills with those of a native speaker.

CONTENTS

Before You Read

Pip

My parents died when I was very young, so I went to live with my older sister and her husband, Joe. Joe is kind and I love him as a father. One day, Someone took an interest in me and is paying for my education to be a proper British gentleman. I wonder who this person is.

Estella

I was raised by Miss Havisham who took me in when I was very little. I am very beautiful and many men want to be with me. However, Miss Havisham taught me how to be cruel to men.

Miss Havisham

I'm an old lady. I have hated all men and can't stand to see couples who love each other.

Joe

I am a blacksmith for this village. Pip is my brother-in-law, but he is so young that my wife and I care for him like he was our son.

Magwitch

I was a prisoner but I managed to escape twice. The first time, I met Pip. The second time I escaped, I went to Australia to become a sheep farmer. I became very wealthy.

Biddy

I am a part-time teacher in the village. When Joe's wife became sick, I moved into their house to take care of her.

Chapter One

🎧 1   # Pip and Estella

My story begins when I was seven years old. I was in the graveyard[1] of the church that was very close to my home. Both of my parents were buried there.

Suddenly I started crying because I felt afraid and the noise of my sobs[2] filled the graveyard.

"Who is making that awful[3] noise[4]?" said a low voice. A terrible looking man came toward me.

"Don't move or I'll cut your throat[5]," he said. He was dirty and was wearing leg irons[6]. He must have[7] escaped[8] from the local[9] prison!

He grabbed[10] me and I cried, "Please don't kill me!"

"What's your name? Quickly!" he demanded[11].

"Pip," I said.

"Where is your home?" he asked. I pointed[12] to the nearby village.

He then turned me upside down[13] to empty[14] my pockets. I only had a piece of bread and he quickly picked it up and devoured[15] it.

1. **graveyard** [ˋɡreɪvˌjɑːrd] (n.) 墓地
2. **sob** [sɑːb] (n.) 嗚咽；啜泣（聲）
3. **awful** [ˋɑːfəl] (a.) 可怕的；嚇人的
4. **noise** [nɔɪz] (n.) 躁音
5. **throat** [θroʊt] (n.) 喉嚨
6. **leg irons** 腳鐐
7. **must have** + 過去分詞 絕對已經
8. **escape** [ɪˋskeɪp] (v.) 逃脫
9. **local** [ˋloʊkəl] (a.) 當地的
10. **grab** [ɡræb] (v.) 抓住 (grab-grabbed-grabbed)
11. **demand** [dɪˋmænd] (v.) 查問；盤問
12. **point** [pɔɪnt] (v.) 指；指出
13. **upside down** 顛倒
14. **empty** [ˋempti] (v.) 倒空
15. **devour** [dɪˋvaʊr] (v.) 狼吞虎嚥；吃光

"Where are your parents?" he asked.
I pointed to the gravestones[1] in the
churchyard.

"They are in the ground over there, sir,"
I replied.

"So who do you live with?"

"My sister, sir. Wife of Joe Gargery, the
blacksmith[2], sir," I told him.

"Blacksmith, eh? You know what a file[3] is?"

"Yes, sir," I said.

"Then you bring me a file and some food
and then I won't kill you," he said.

I agreed and then he let me go.

Just before I left he said again, "You bring
me the file and food tonight, you hear. And
don't tell anyone you saw me. If you do, I'll
find you and tear[4] your heart and liver[5] out."

1. **gravestone** [ˋgreɪvˌstoun]
   (n.) 墓碑
2. **blacksmith** [ˋblækˌsmɪθ]
   (n.) 鐵匠；工匠
3. **file** [faɪl] (n.) 銼刀
4. **tear A out** 把A 撕扯出來
   (tear-tore-torn)
5. **liver** [ˋlɪvər] (n.) 肝臟
6. **absolutely** [ˌæbsəˋluːtli]
   (adv.) 完全地
7. **terrify** [ˋterəfaɪ] (v.) 使害怕
8. **keep quiet** 保持安靜
9. **flee** [fliː] (v.) 逃走
   (flee-fled-fled)

I was absolutely[6] terrified[7] so, once more, I promised to bring the things and to keep quiet[8]. Then I fled[9] from the graveyard.

I thought, "I have to bring him what he wants. If I don't, he might find me at home and kill me. He knows where I live."

I was worried. It would not be easy to sneak[1] the food out of the house. My sister was much older than me and often lost her temper[2]. If she caught me, she would punish[3] me. On the other hand[4], her husband Joe was always kind to me. He often protected[5] me from my sister.

That night, when I tried to hide[6] some bread in my pocket, he said, "Pip! You are eating too fast. You couldn't have eaten all your bread so quickly! You'll get sick[7] if you're not careful."

My sister looked at me and said, "What's he been doing?"

"He's eating too quickly. I ate too quickly when I was a boy but not as fast as you!" Joe said.

1. **sneak** [sniːk] (v.)
   偷偷取得；偷竊
2. **lose one's temper**
   發脾氣；情緒失控
3. **punish** [ˋpʌnɪʃ] (v.)
   懲罰；處罰
4. **on the other hand**
   另一方面
5. **protect A from B**
   保護 A 不受 B（的傷害）
6. **hide** [haɪd] (v.) 隱藏
   (hide-hid-hid)
7. **get sick** 生病
8. **pull A up by**
   用……把A拉上來
9. **dose** [dous] (v.) 服藥

My sister pulled[8] me up from the table by
my hair.

"Well, then! It's time for a dosing[9]!" My
sister made me drink a spoonful[10] of 'tar[11]
water' which was a disgusting[12], thick[13], dark
liquid[14]. It was awful. I swallowed[15] it as
quickly as I could.

10. **spoonful** [`spuːnfʊl] (n.)
    滿滿一匙的量
11. **tar** [tɑːr] (n.) 焦油
12. **disgusting** [dɪs`gʌstɪŋ] (a.)
    令人作嘔的
13. **thick** [θɪk] (a.)
    濃稠的；混濁的
14. **liquid** [`lɪkwɪd] (n.) 液體
15. **swallow** [`swɑːloʊ] (v.)
    吞；嚥

When Joe and my sister were asleep[1], I crept into[2] the kitchen and grabbed a pork[3] pie from the pantry[4]. Joe's Uncle Pumblechook had given it to my sister for Christmas dinner which was the next day. After that, I took some brandy[5], and a file from Joe's workshop[6]. I ran to the graveyard and quickly gave the pie, brandy and file to the awful man. He was very happy. Then I ran back home.

The next day came and I was very worried. I knew my sister would discover that the pie and brandy were gone.

My sister prepared dinner and Uncle Pumblechook and another man, Mr. Wopsle, came to have dinner with us. It was a very nice dinner and near the end I began to think I might survive[7] the night.

Just then, my sister said, "I almost forgot. Uncle Pumblechook gave us a pie." She went to get it but came back empty-handed[8].

"It's gone!" she said in a surprised voice.

I felt so guilty[9] that I jumped up and ran out of the room. I ran to the front door[10] and opened it. I was very surprised. There was a group of soldiers and a policeman standing in front of the door.

1. **asleep** [ə`sliːp] (a.) 睡著的
2. **creep into**
   躡手躡腳地走進……
   (creep-crept-crept)
3. **pork** [pɔːrk] (n.) 豬肉
4. **pantry** [`pæntri] (n.)
   餐具室；食品儲藏室
5. **brandy** [`brændi] (n.)
   白蘭地酒
6. **workshop** [`wɜːrkˌʃɑːp] (n.)
   工場；小工廠
7. **survive** [sər`vaɪv] (v.)
   從……逃生；倖存
8. **empty-handed**
   空手的；一無所有的
9. **feel guilty** 覺得有罪惡感
   (guilty: 有罪的；內疚的)
10. **front door** 正門；大門

19

The policeman said, "We need Joe to fix[1] these for us." He was holding some handcuffs[2]. "Two prisoners escaped from the prison last night."

Joe took the handcuffs and repaired[3] them. Then, we all went to join in[4] the search[5] for the two men. I sat high on Joe's shoulders as we walked through fields and forests. I hoped I would see the prisoner first. I was afraid that he would think I had told the police about him.

After some more searching, we all heard shouting. We followed the noise and saw two men fighting. One was the prisoner I gave food to and the other had a long scar[6] on his face. The soldiers quickly caught them.

1. **fix** [fɪks] (v.) 修理
2. **handcuffs** [ˋhændkʌfs] (n.) 手銬
3. **repair** [rɪˋper] (v.) 修理
4. **join in** 參加
5. **search** [sɜːrtʃ] (n.) 搜查；搜尋
6. **scar** [skɑːr] (n.) 疤；傷痕
7. **lead away** 帶走
8. **shake one's head** ……搖頭 (shake-shook-shaken)
9. **keep one's promise** 遵守……承諾
10. **anger** [ˋæŋgər] (n.) 生氣；發怒
11. **steal** [stiːl] (v.) 偷竊 (steal-stole-stolen)
12. **miss** [mɪs] (v.) 不見；丟失
13. **right** [raɪt] (n.) 權利

As they were led away[7], the man I had met saw me. I shook my head[8]. I was trying to tell him that I had kept my promise[9]. He looked at me without anger[10].

He turned to the policeman and said, "I stole[11] a pork pie and some brandy from the blacksmith's."

Joe said in a surprised voice, "Yes, we are missing[12] a pork pie." Joe then said to the prisoner, "Whatever wrong thing you did, you have a right[13] to eat."

Then the soldiers took the two prisoners back to prison.

In the village, I was going to an elementary school[1]. Mr. Wopsle's great-aunt[2] taught at the school. She was very old and she often fell asleep in class[3]. She had a granddaughter, Biddy, and she sometimes taught in the school instead of her grandmother. She was an orphan[4] and even though she looked a little dirty, she was very kind to all of the students. She taught me to read and write.

One cold winter evening, I sat beside Joe and wrote on a slate[5]:

"MI DEER JO i OPE U R gRWrTE WELL i OpE i SHAL soN B HhBELL 42 TEEDGE U JO"

("My dear Joe, I hope you are quite well. I hope I shall soon be able to teach you, Joe.")

1. **elementary school** 小學
2. **great-aunt**
   伯母；姑婆；舅媽
   (=grandaunt)
3. **in class** 在課堂上
4. **orphan** [ˋɔːrfən] (n.) 孤兒
5. **slate** [sleɪt] (n.) 石板
6. **impressed** [ɪmˋprest] (a.)
   印象深刻的
7. **exclaim** [ɪkˋskleɪm] (v.)
   驚呼
8. **dream of** 夢想
9. **all day long** 整天
10. **interrupt** [ˌɪntəˋrʌpt] (v.)
    打斷（談話或講話的人）
11. **pamper** [ˋpæmpər] (v.)
    寵溺；縱容

Joe was very impressed[6] with my note.

"Pip! How smart you are!" he exclaimed[7].
He smiled at me.

Joe had promised to teach me to become a blacksmith when I became older. But I didn't want this. I dreamed of[8] a better life. I wanted to be rich and to study all day long[9]. I sat dreaming about the life I wanted but my happy thoughts were interrupted[10] when my sister came into the room saying, "Well, what a lucky boy our Pip is! I hope she doesn't pamper[11] him."

Mr. Pumblechook was with my sister and he said, "She's not the type[1] to pamper a person."

"Who?" asked Joe.

"Miss Havisham," replied my sister impatiently[2]. "She wants Pip to play with a girl in her house. She might even pay him. He'd better[3] go or he'll be in trouble with[4] me."

Joe was very surprised. "How does she know Pip?" he asked.

"Idiot[5]!" replied my sister. "She doesn't know him! Uncle Pumblechook is her neighbor. She asked if he knew a boy and then he kindly[6] mentioned[7] Pip."

1. **type** [taɪp] (n.)
   具有某種特點的人
2. **impatiently** [ɪmˋpeɪʃəntli]
   (adv.) 不耐煩地
3. **'d (=had) better**+原形動詞
   最好……
4. **be in trouble with**
   和……一起會有麻煩
5. **idiot** [ˋɪdiət] (n.)
   白痴；笨蛋
6. **kindly** [ˋkaɪndli] (adv.)
   親切地；好心地
7. **mention** [ˋmenʃən] (v.)
   提起；提到
8. **pleased** [pliːzd] (a.)
   高興的
9. **grateful** [ˋgreɪtfəl] (a.)
   感激的；感謝的
10. **stern** [stɜːrn] (a.)
    嚴格的；苛刻的

Uncle Pumblechook looked very pleased[8]. He was proud he knew Miss Havisham.

"This boy could make money by going to Miss Havisham. He should be grateful[9]," said my sister.

I was not grateful at all. Miss Havisham was a very rich but strange and stern[10] woman. She lived in a large, cold house and she never went outside. I didn't want to spend any time with her or in her house. But I had no choice but to go.

🎧 8

The next morning, my sister forced me to[1] leave the house with Uncle Pumblechook. We walked slowly to Miss Havisham's house. We rang the bell[2] and a servant[3] opened the gate.

She let me in[4] but said to Uncle Pumblechook, "She doesn't want to see you!"

I followed the servant through the dark, dreary[5] house until we came to a door. The servant knocked on the door[6] and said, "Go in!" I entered and the door was slammed[7] behind me.

There were many candles in the room and Miss Havisham was sitting in a chair. She was dressed completely[8] in white[9] and wore many jewels[10]. She had a veil[11] over her face. She was the strangest looking person I had ever seen.

1. **force A to** 強迫 A 去……
2. **ring a bell** 按門鈴 (ring-rang-rung)
3. **servant** [ˈsɜːrvənt] (n.) 僕人；佣人
4. **let A in** 讓 A 進入
5. **dreary** [ˈdrɪri] (a.) 陰鬱的；沈悶的
6. **knock on the door** 敲門
7. **slam** [slæm] (v.) 猛地關上
8. **completely** [kəmˈpliːtli] (adv.) 完全地；徹底地
9. **dress in white** 穿著白色衣服
10. **jewel** [ˈdʒuːəl] (n.) 寶石
11. **veil** [veɪl] (n.) 面紗

"Who is it?" she demanded.

"I am Pip, Ma'am[1]," I said.

"Pip?"

"Yes, Ma'am! Mr. Pumblechook's boy. I've come to play," I told her.

"Come here," she said.

I was extremely[2] scared[3] but I walked closer. I saw her watch. It was twenty minutes to nine. Also, the clock on the wall had stopped at the same time.

1. **ma'am** [mæm] (n.) 女士
2. **extremely** [ɪk`striːmli] (adv.) 非常；極其
3. **scared** [skerd] (a.) 嚇壞的；恐懼的
4. **chest** [tʃest] (n.) 胸；胸膛
5. **broken** [`broʊkən] (v.) 被打碎的
6. **name** [neɪm] (v.) 命名
7. **call out** 大聲叫喊
8. **figure** [`fɪgjər] (n.) 人影
9. **walk along . . .** 沿著……走
10. **walk over to . . .** 走到……

She said to me, "Are you afraid of a woman who has not seen the sun for many, many years?" Then, she put her hand on her chest[4]. "Do you know what is in here?" she asked me.

"Your heart," I said. "Yes, and it's broken[5]," she cried. Then she said, "A girl named[6] Estella lives here. I want you to play with her. Go and call her."

I went to the door and called out[7] for Estella. I waited and then shouted out again. Finally, I saw a small figure[8] walking along[9] the hall. She entered the room and walked over to[10] Miss Havisham.

"I want to see you play cards[1] with this boy," she said to Estella.

"With him?" the girl asked. Her pretty face soured[2] with scorn[3]. "He is just a common[4] working boy!"

Miss Havisham whispered[5] something into her ear.

"You can make him fall in love with[6] you and then break his heart[7]."

Estella finally sat down and dealt the cards[8]. I picked up my cards and she looked at my hands.

---

1. **play cards** 玩紙牌遊戲
2. **sour** [saur] (v.)
   變得不愉快
3. **scorn** [skɔːrn] (n.)
   輕蔑；藐視
4. **common** [ˈkɑːmən] (a.)
   普通的；常見的
5. **whisper** [ˈwɪspər] (v.)
   低語；耳語

6. **fall in love with** 愛上……
7. **break one's heart**
   傷了……的心
8. **deal cards** 發牌
   (deal-dealt-dealt)
9. **rough** [rʌf] (a.) 粗糙的
10. **clumsy** [ˈklʌmzi] (a.)
   笨拙的；不靈活的

"He has such rough[9] hands and thick boots. He looks stupid and clumsy[10]!" she said.

I had never been ashamed of[11] myself before but I looked at my hands and boots. My clothes were dirty and my hair was tangled[12]. She looked down on[13] me as though I was dirt[14] on her shoe.

We continued to play and she won. After that, I dealt the cards for a second game. She made me feel very nervous[15] and so I made a mistake.

"You are so stupid. Don't you know anything?" she snapped[16] at me.

She was very unkind but I didn't say anything back to her.

11. **be ashamed of**
為……感到難為情
12. **tangled** ['tæŋɡld] (a.)
糾纏的
13. **look down on** 輕視……

14. **dirt** [dɜːrt] (n.) 爛泥；灰塵
15. **nervous** ['nɜːrvəs] (a.)
神經質的；緊張不安的
16. **snap** [snæp] (v.)
厲聲說

"Why didn't you defend[1] yourself?" asked Miss Havisham. "She says many mean[2] things to you. What do you think of her? Whisper in my ear." I stood up and went to her.

I whispered, "I think she is very proud[3]."

"Really? Anything else?" she asked.

"I think she is very pretty."

Estella heard me say this and she wasn't pleased.

"Anything else?" Miss Havisham asked again.

"She is very insulting[4]," I replied. "And I would like to[5] go home."

1. **defend** [dɪˋfɛnd] (v.) 為……辯護
2. **mean** [miːn] (a.) 邪惡的
3. **proud** [praʊd] (a.) 驕傲的
4. **insulting** [ɪnˋsʌltɪŋ] (a.) 侮辱人的；無理的
5. **would like to . . .** 想要……
6. **let A out** 讓 A 出去
7. **look** [lʊk] (n.) 表情；臉色
8. **disgust** [dɪsˋgʌst] (n.) 作嘔；厭惡
9. **kick** [kɪk] (v.) 踢
10. **courtyard** [ˋkɔːrtˏjɑːrd] (n.) 庭院
11. **get in** 進入……
12. **take off** 脫下
13. **fist** [fɪst] (n.) 拳
14. **bravely** [ˋbreɪvli] (adv.) 勇敢地；英勇地
15. **victorious** [vɪkˋtɔːriəs] (a.) 勝利的
16. **sadden** [ˋsædən] (v.) 使悲傷；使難過

Estella took me to the front door and let me out[6]. As she closed the door, I saw her face. She gave me a look[7] of disgust[8]. I felt very sad and started crying. I kicked[9] a wall in the courtyard[10] and then I saw a tall, thin boy.

"How did you get in[11]?" he asked.

"Estella let me in."

"Come and fight me," he demanded. He took off[12] his coat and put his fists[13] up. I was afraid of him but I hit him two times in the face and he fell to the ground.

"You won," he said, bravely[14]. I didn't feel victorious[15]. Estella had saddened[16] my life.

The Gentlemen in the Victorian Age

Before the Victorian Age in England, Pip's change from blacksmith's apprentice to English gentleman would have been impossible. A person's position in society was determined by their birth. Sons and daughters did what their fathers and mothers did.

However, in the Victorian Age, people who inherited a lot of money, or worked very hard, could raise their status.

To be a proper English gentleman, Pip had to have money. Once he got this money, he then needed to be educated in academic subjects like History and Literature.

He also had to learn how to behave. This included learning the proper way to speak, greet others, dress, eat his meals and all sorts of other everyday activities. This is why he went to study with Mr. Pocket.

A gentleman was considered as part of the upper class and was expected to behave as a refined person. Of course, not all gentlemen learned how to behave well, as in the case of Drummle.

· Chapter Two ·

🎧12 A Change of Fortune[1]

The next few months were mixed with[2] pain[3] and pleasure. Every day, I went to Miss Havisham's house to play with Estella. Every day, she was very mean to me. But despite[4] her cruelty[5], I was captivated[6] by her and I wanted to see her. Also, Miss Havisham spoke to me more and more as she got used to[7] me.

1. **fortune** [ˋfɔːrtʃən] (n.) 命運
2. **be mixed with** 摻雜著……
3. **pain** [peɪn] (n.) 痛苦；煩惱
4. **despite** [dɪˋspaɪt] (prep.) 儘管
5. **cruelty** [ˋkruːəltɪ] (n.) 殘酷；殘忍
6. **captivate** [ˋkæptəˌveɪt] (v.) 使著迷
7. **get used to** 習慣於……

One day, she asked me to push her in her wheelchair into the room next door. The room was dark and dusty[8] and there were cobwebs[9] everywhere.

There was a long table. On it was a wedding feast[10]. Mice and rats[11] were chewing[12] on the rotten[13] cake in the middle. However the room did not surprise me at all[14] as Miss Havisham was a strange woman.

8. **dusty** [`dʌsti] (a.)
   滿是灰塵的
9. **cobweb** [`kɑːb‚web] (n.)
   蜘蛛網
10. **feast** [fiːst] (n.) 盛宴；筵席

11. **rat** [ræt] (n.) 鼠
12. **chew** [tʃuː] (v.) 咀嚼
13. **rotten** [`rɑːtn] (a.)
    腐爛；發臭的
14. **not . . . at all** 一點也不

🎧 13

One day, Miss Havisham asked me, "What do you want to do when you are older?"

I replied, "I will become Joe's apprentice[1]. I don't want to though[2]. I want to be a gentleman and read books all day."

Secretly[3] I thought to myself, "I hope Miss Havisham helps me to become a gentleman."

But she never did. She only gave me dinner for playing with Estella.

She said, "I want you to bring Joe with you tomorrow. You are growing up[4] and it's time for you to learn your life's work."

The next day, Joe came with me to Miss Havisham's house.

1. **apprentice** [ə`prentɪs] (n.) 學徒；徒弟
2. **though** [ðou] (adv.) 雖然
3. **secretly** [`si:krɪtli] (adv.) 秘密地；背地裡
4. **grow up** 成長

5. **correct** [kə`rekt] (a.) 正確的；對的
6. **laugh at** 嘲笑
7. **fine** [faɪn] (a.) 傑出的；優秀的
8. **one day** （將來）有一天
9. **with that** 接著；然後

"Is it correct[5] that this boy is to become your apprentice?" she asked Joe.

"You want to work with me, don't you Pip?" Joe asked me.

I felt very ashamed, especially when I saw Estella laughing at[6] me.

Miss Havisham said, "I want you to be Mr. Gargery's apprentice. Here is some money. Give this money to Mr. Gargery. You will be a fine[7] blacksmith one day[8]."

With that[9], my visits to the house ended and I started to learn how to be a blacksmith. I was very unhappy, however, and I worried that Estella would one day see my face covered in black and look at me in disgust again.

I worked with Joe and the time passed by quickly.

One year later, I asked Joe if I could visit Miss Havisham.

"Is that a good idea?" he replied. "Because she might think you want something."

"But I've never thanked her for what she did. We aren't busy these days. Can I take half a day[1] to see Miss Est-Havisham?" I asked.

Joe said, smiling, "Her name isn't Esthavisham!"

Joe finally agreed but then Orlick, Joe's other worker, wanted some time off[2] too. My sister told Joe not to give Orlick any time off. My sister and Orlick were always fighting. She thought he was lazy. But Joe allowed him to take the time off anyway.

1. **take half a day**
   花費半天的時間
2. **off** [ɒːf] (a.)
   休假的；不上班的
3. **put on** 穿上

4. **set off for . . .**
   出發去……；起身去……
5. **admire** [ədˋmaɪr] (v.) 欣賞
6. **depressed** [dɪˋprɛst] (a.)
   沮喪的；消沈的

I was excited to see Estella again. I washed
and put on[3] my best clothes. I happily set off
for[4] Miss Havisham's house. When I arrived,
I was very disappointed.

"Estella is in Europe," Miss Havisham told
me. "She is getting an education. She is even
more beautiful now. Everyone admires[5] her so
much."

I left Miss Havisham's house feeling very
depressed[6]. I really felt I had lost Estella now.

I walked home. It was very dark and there was a heavy[1] mist[2]. I could hear the sound of guns in the distance[3]. On the way, I met Orlick.

He said, "Some prisoners have escaped from the prison again."

I remembered the night long ago when I had met the escaped prisoner in the graveyard.

As I was nearing[4] home, a neighbor ran to me and said, "A prisoner broke into[5] your house and someone was attacked[6]."

I ran home to find a crowd[7] in the yard[8]. Joe and a doctor were in the kitchen. My sister was lying on the floor. She had been hit many times on her head and back. Beside her were some leg irons.

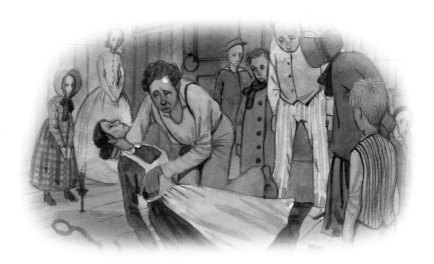

"The irons had been cut through[9] many years before," Joe said.

They were the irons my prisoner had cut through! But I knew he hadn't attacked my sister. The attacker must have found the irons in the graveyard and then brought them into the house. Only Orlick could have done this. No one else hated my sister, but there was nothing to prove[10] he had done it.

1. **heavy** [`hevi] (a.)
   陰沈的;沈重的
2. **mist** [mɪst] (n.) 霧
3. **in the distance**
   在(相當)遠處
4. **near** [nɪr] (v.) 接近
5. **break into** 闖入……

6. **attack** [ə`tæk] (v.)
   攻擊;襲擊
7. **crowd** [kraʊd] (n.) 人群
8. **yard** [jɑːrd] (n.) 院子;庭院
9. **cut through** 切斷
10. **prove** [pruːv] (v.) 證明

I had a terrible feeling of guilt[1]. I felt responsible[2] because I provided[3] the weapon.

My sister lived but she changed a lot. In some ways, it was good because she never yelled[4] again or became impatient. But she never spoke again either and was sometimes unhappy.

Biddy came to live with us to help take care of my sister. She was clever and kind, but not as beautiful as Estella. I wished I could fall in love with her but my heart belonged to[5] Estella.

My life continued as normal with me working with Joe for the next four years.

One day, a man named Mr. Jaggers, who was a lawyer, came to visit with some news. This changed my life forever.

"Mr. Gargery, my client wants to take this young man and raise him as a gentleman. You will be paid for your loss[6], of course," Mr. Jaggers said.

Joe replied, "That is not necessary. If Pip has come into[7] some good fortune[8], I won't stop him."

I was thunderstruck[9]. My dreams had come true[10]! I was so happy but I felt guilty to leave Joe who had always been so kind to me.

1. **guilt** [gɪlt] (n.) 罪惡感
2. **responsible** [rɪ`spɑ:nsəbəl] (a.) 需負責任的
3. **provide** [prə`vaɪd] (v.) 提供
4. **yell** [jel] (v.) 叫喊；吼叫
5. **belong to** 屬於
6. **loss** [lɒ:s] (n.) 損失；虧損
7. **come into** 繼承
8. **fortune** [`fɔ:rtʃən] (n.) 財富
9. **thunderstruck** [`θʌndər͵strʌk] (a.) 嚇壞了的；嚇呆了
10. **dreams come true** 夢想成真

🎧 17

Mr. Jaggers continued, "There are two conditions[1] for this gift. You must keep the name Pip and your benefactor's[2] name must be a secret. Here is some money. Buy some new clothes. You will go to London in one week to live with Mr. Pocket and his son Herbert."

"The Pockets!" I thought. "They are relatives[3] of Miss Havisham. She must be my benefactor."

"Here is my business card[4]. When you arrive in London, please come to this address," Mr. Jaggers said and then he left.

Joe and I went into the house immediately to tell my sister and Biddy about my good fortune.

Joe ran in first and exclaimed, "Well! The strangest things happen. God has blessed[5] our Pip and he is now a gentleman of fortune."

The two women looked at me in amazement[6].

"Congratulations[7], Pip!" Biddy said. But there was a sadness in their eyes that made me angry.

I thought, "Why can't they both be more happy for me?"

1. **condition** [kənˈdɪʃən] (n.) 條件
2. **benefactor** [ˈbenɪfæktər] (n.) 捐助人；恩人
3. **relative** [ˈrelətɪv] (n.) 親戚
4. **business card** 名片
5. **bless** [bles] (v.) 為……祝福；保佑
6. **in amazement** 驚訝地
7. **Congratulations!** [kənˌgrætʃuˈleɪʃənz] 恭喜

At dinner that night, they all kept congratulating[1, 2] me. But it seemed so unreal[3] to them all and it made me feel very strange.

I couldn't understand it. I had come into such great fortune but I felt lonelier[4] than ever[5].

That night, I thought of Estella. "What if [6] Miss Havisham wants me to marry Estella?" I thought. This made me feel very happy.

The next day, I ordered the finest clothes. They were very expensive and I proudly showed them off [7] to Joe and Biddy.

"I will go and say good-bye[8] to Miss Havisham," I said to them.

1. **keep + V-ing** 持續……
2. **congratulate** [kənˋgrætʃuleɪt] (v.) 祝賀；恭喜
3. **unreal** [ʌnˋrɪəl] (a.) 不真實的；假的
4. **lonely** [ˋlounli] (a.) 孤獨的；單獨的
5. **ever** [ˋevər] (adv.) 在任何時候；從來；至今
6. **What if . . .?** 如果……？

When I arrived, I said to her, "I have just come into a great fortune, Miss Havisham. I am especially grateful for it."

"Yes, I heard from Mr. Jaggers about it. You have been adopted[9] by a rich person, I hear," Miss Havisham said.

"Yes, Ma'am," I replied.

"And you have no idea who it is?" she asked me.

"No, Ma'am," I said, making sure[10] not to say that I thought she was my benefactor.

"Well, then! Your future looks very secure[11] now. I wish you the best of luck and I hope you will always keep the name Pip," she said. "Good-bye, Pip."

I kneeled[12] in front of her and kissed her hand as a way of thanking her for everything she had done for me.

7. **show off** 賣弄;炫耀
8. **say good-bye**
   道別;說再見
9. **adopt** [əˋdɑːpt] (v.)
   收養;過繼
10. **make sure**
    設法確保
11. **secure** [sɪˋkjʊr] (a.)
    安全的;安妥的
12. **kneel** [niːl] (v.) 跪下

The day came for me to leave for London. I was very excited and very nervous at the same time. I was greatly looking forward to[1] my life as a gentleman. I ate my breakfast very quickly and then I kissed my sister and Biddy good-bye. I put my arms around Joe and then I left.

I walked into the village to catch the coach[2]. If I had boarded[3] the coach in front of Joe's old house, I would have been very embarrassed[4]. I was filled with mixed feelings. As I left the village, tears rolled down[5] my cheeks.

"Good-bye, Joe," I thought. "Good-bye, my dearest[6] friend!"

I felt terrible at the thought of leaving such a wonderful and kind man. Yet my heart was also rejoicing[7]. My new and exciting life was just beginning.

1. **look forward to**（＋名詞）
   盼望……

2. **coach** [koutʃ] (n.)
   大馬車；公共馬車

3. **board** [bɔːrd] (v.)
   上（船車、飛機等）

4. **embarrassed** [ɪmˋbærəst]
   (a.) 窘的；尷尬的

5. **roll down** 流下；滾下

6. **dear** [dɪr] (a.)
   親愛的；可愛的

7. **rejoice** [rɪˋdʒɔɪs] (v.)
   欣喜；高興

A True or False.

T F ➊ Miss Havisham's wedding feast had been prepared many years ago.

T F ➋ Miss Havisham gave Pip some money to become a writer.

T F ➌ Pip's sister thought that Orlick worked very hard.

T F ➍ Pip suspected that Orlick attacked his sister.

T F ➎ Mr. Jaggers went to Pip to tell him he wanted to be his benefactor.

B Fill in the blanks with "a/an" or "the".

After some more searching, we all heard ➊ _____ noise. We followed ➋ _____ noise and saw two men fighting. One was ➌ _____ prisoner I gave food to and ➍ _____ other had ➎ _____ long scar on his face. ➏ _____ soldiers quickly caught them. ➐ _____ man I had met saw me. I was trying to tell him that I hadn't told ➑ _____ police about him. He looked at me without anger. He turned to ➒ _____ policeman and said, "I stole ➓ _____ pork pie and some brandy from ⑪ _____ blacksmith's."

C Choose the correct answer.

1 Why didn't Pip want to become a blacksmith?

(a) Because he wanted to become a carpenter.

(b) Because he wanted to become a gentleman.

(c) Because he wanted to visit Estella every day.

2 How did Miss Havisham pay Pip for playing with Estella?

(a) She bought him new clothes.

(b) She paid him money each day.

(c) She gave him dinner every day.

D Fill in the blanks with the given words.

disturbed	clever	impressed
wealthy	imagined	

I had written the message to Joe and he was very

1 _____. "Pip! How **2** _____ you are!" he exclaimed.
He smiled at me. Later on, when I was older, he was going
to teach me to become a blacksmith. But I didn't want to.
I **3** _____ a better life. I wanted to be
4 _____ and to study all day long. I sat dreaming about
the life I wanted but my happy thoughts were
5 _____ when my sister came into the room.

Chapter Three

 20 A New Beginning

My journey[1] to London was a very pleasant one. Even though the trip took five hours, the time went by[2] very quickly. It was just after twelve o'clock in the afternoon when I finally arrived.

The driver of the coach took me to Mr. Jaggers' office. It was not quite[3] what I had expected[4]. The building was rather old and gray-looking[5].

I went into the office and asked the clerk[6], "I have come to see Mr. Jaggers."

The clerk replied, "He is in court[7] at the moment[8]. Are you Mr. Pip?"

"Yes, I am," I said.

"We have been waiting for you to arrive. Mr. Jaggers told me to take you to your new home if you arrived while he was away," the clerk told me.

He then got his coat and hat and we left the building.

1. **journey** [ˈdʒɜːrni] (n.) 旅行
2. **go by** （時間）過去
3. **quite** [kwaɪt] (adv.) 完全地
4. **expect** [ɪkˈspɛkt] (v.) 期待；預期
5. **gray-looking** 外表陰暗的
6. **clerk** [klɜːrk] (n.) 辦事員；職員
7. **court** [kɔːrt] (n.) 法庭
8. **at the moment** 此刻；當時

21

He took me to a very nice little house. On the mail box, I could see the name, "Mr. Pocket, Junior[1]."

"This is it. You can just go in and wait in the living room," he said.

I went up the front stairs and entered the house. I went into the living room and not long after[2], I heard someone walking up the steps[3]. A young man a little older than me entered the room. He was carrying some grocery[4] bags.

He looked at me and asked, "Are you Mr. Pip?"

"Yes, I am," I replied. "Are you Mr. Herbert Pocket?"

We looked into each other's faces. He looked very familiar[5] to me.

"We've met before," he told me. "You're the boy I fought and who knocked me to the ground[6] in Miss Havisham's courtyard."

I remembered now and said, "Yes, of course!" We both laughed.

1. **Junior** [`dʒuːniər]
   小（置於姓名後表示同名父子中的子或年幼者）
2. **not long after** 沒多久後
3. **step** [step] (n.) 台階
4. **grocery** [`grousəri] (n.)
   食品雜貨
5. **familiar** [fə`mɪliər] (a.)
   熟悉的

"I heard about your good news," Herbert told me. "I still remember so clearly[7] when we first met. Like you, I had been invited to play with Estella. But Miss Havisham didn't like me. It turned out[8] that she liked you more. It was actually[9] good because she's a nightmare[10]."

6. **knock A to the ground**
   把A擊倒
7. **clearly** [ˋklɪrli] (adv.)
   清晰地;清楚地
8. **turn out**
   結果是……
9. **actually** [ˋæktʃuəli] (adv.)
   實際上;真的
10. **nightmare** [ˋnaɪtmɛr] (n.)
   夢魘;惡夢

22

"Who do you mean[1]? Miss Havisham?"
I asked, confused[2].

"No, no! Estella. Miss Havisham taught her
to hate men," he said. "Do you know the story
about Miss Havisham?"

"No," I replied.

"I'll tell you later over[3] dinner," Herbert
promised.

For the rest of the afternoon, I settled[4] into
my new room. Dinner time came and just as
he had promised, Herbert told me about Miss
Havisham.

"Miss Havisham's father was a very rich
man. He was married twice and with his first
wife, he had a daughter, Miss Havisham, and
with the second wife, he had a son. The son
was a terrible person and so Mr. Havisham
gave most of his money to Miss Havisham."

1. **mean** [miːn] (v.) 意指
2. **confused** [kənˋfjuːzd] (a.)
　 困惑的
3. **over** [ˋouvər] (prep.)
　 在⋯⋯期間
4. **settle** [ˋsetl] (v.)
　 安頓；定居

"Miss Havisham's half-brother[5] was extremely[6] jealous[7]. He asked a friend to pretend[8] to fall in love with her and ask her to marry him. She agreed and prepared everything for the wedding. However, he never showed up[9] for the wedding. Instead, she received a letter from him saying that he would never marry her."

Then I said, "That must be why all of her clocks have stopped at twenty minutes to nine. She must have received the letter at that time."

"Yes, that's right," agreed Herbert. "She stopped all of the clocks just then and never went out of the house again."

"Well, do you know how Estella came to live with Miss Havisham?" I asked him.

"I have no idea," he replied.

5. **half-brother**
   同父異母（或同母異父）
   的兄弟

6. **extremely** [ɪk`striːmli]
   (adv.) 極端地；非常

7. **jealous** [`dʒeləs] (a.)
   妒忌的

8. **pretend** [prɪ`tend] (v.)
   假裝；佯裝

9. **show up** 露面；出席

Later, I went to bed and awoke to a bright[1] new morning. The next day, Herbert's father started teaching me to become a gentleman. He was a wonderful teacher and he gave me so many books to read.

I read adventure and mystery[2] stories as well as[3] essays, comedies[4] and even plays[5]. We often went shopping together and he helped me to develop[6] a good sense of style. He taught me how to dress and how to behave[7] at parties. Herbert was a wonderful teacher too. He taught me table manners[8] and he was always a great example for me to follow.

I was not the only person Mr. Pocket was teaching. There were two other students. One student was named Startop. We became very good friends. I found him to be very warm and friendly and we often went rowing[9] together.

The other student was named Bentley Drummle. I did not like him at all and neither did Startop. He had a very mean personality[10] and was very proud and lazy.

1. **bright** [braɪt] (a.)
   晴朗的；明亮的
2. **mystery** [ˋmɪstəri] (n.)
   懸疑故事
3. **as well as** 以及
4. **comedy** [ˋkɑːmədi] (n.)
   喜劇
5. **play** [pleɪ] (n.) 劇本
6. **develop** [dɪˋveləp] (v.)
   發展
7. **behave** [bɪˋheɪv] (v.)
   表現；行為舉止
8. **table manners** 餐桌禮儀
9. **go rowing** 去划船
10. **personality**
    [͵pɝːsəˋnæləti] (n.)
    人格；人品

24

One day, Mr. Jaggers invited my fellow[1] students and me for dinner.

Startop, Drummle, and I met at Jaggers's house and Mr. Jaggers kindly took us into his dining room[2].

Mr. Jaggers asked, "Who are these fine men with you this evening, Pip?"

I introduced Startop and Drummle. I was very surprised because Mr. Jaggers seemed to like Drummle very much.

We all sat down to dinner and the first course[3] was served[4] by a woman who looked about forty years old. She was very quiet and did her work very efficiently[5]. I didn't know what it was but something seemed very familiar about her.

1. **fellow** [ˋfelou] (a.) 同伴的
2. **dining room** 餐廳
3. **course** [kɔːrs] (n.) 一道菜
4. **serve** [sɜːrv] (v.) 服務；端上
5. **efficiently** [ɪˋfɪʃəntli] (adv.) 高效率地
6. **closely** [ˋklousli] (adv.) 仔細地
7. **a great deal of** 大量的
8. **drink to** 為……乾杯
9. **astounded** [əˋstaʊndɪd] (a.) 被震驚的
10. **fool** [fuːl] (v.) 愚弄；欺騙

Each time she came in with a new course, I closely[6] watched her. I wanted to know why she seemed so familiar to me.

The dinner finally came to an end. During the dinner, Mr. Jaggers and Drummle had had a great deal of[7] conversation.

Mr. Jaggers said, "Mr. Drummle, I drink to[8] you. You will be very successful in life." Startop and I were astounded[9] at this. Mr. Jaggers was a very smart man but he had been fooled[10] by Drummle. Unfortunately, Mr. Jaggers would not be the only one.

25

My life passed by[1] very pleasantly[2] in London. I learned a great deal[3] and spent my days trying to improve[4] myself more and more. One day, I received a letter from Biddy. It read,

> *Dear Mr. Pip,*
>
> *Mr. Gargery asked me to write to you. He plans to go to London and he would like to see you. He will visit you tomorrow morning at nine o'clock.*
>
> > *Biddy*
>
> *P.S.[5] Even though you are now a refined [6] gentleman, please see Mr. Gargery. He is such a kind and gentle man and so are you.*

Even though it was good news that Joe was coming to London, I did not want to see him. I still cared very much for[7] him but he did not fit into[8] my life anymore.

If I could have prevented him from[9] coming to the house, I would have. I felt guilty because I was not kind like Biddy said I was.

The next morning, I got up early to clean and get ready[10] for Joe's visit. Later in the morning, I heard him arrive. I could hear the sound of his heavy clumsy boots on the stairs. I met him at the front door and showed him in[11].

"Joe, it's good to see you. How are you?" I asked him.

"Pip, how are you?" he replied.

1. **pass by**（時間）過去
2. **pleasantly** [ˋplɛzəntli] (adv.) 愉快地；快活地
3. **a great deal** 大量；非常
4. **improve** [ɪmˋpruːv] (v.) 改進；改善
5. **P.S.** = postscript 附言
6. **refined** [rɪˋfaɪnd] (a.) 有教養的；文雅的
7. **care for** 喜歡；照料
8. **fit into** 適合……
9. **prevent A from + V-ing** 防止 A 去做……
10. **get ready** 準備好
11. **show A in** 請 A 進入

26

Joe put his hat on the floor and took both of my hands in his and shook them for the longest time. For a moment I didn't think that he was going to let go[1].

"It's so good to see you, Joe. Give me your hat," I said. Joe felt very awkward[2] in the house and he didn't want to give me his hat. He picked his hat up off the floor and held it very tightly[3] in his hands.

"You've changed so much," he said. "You've grown into a fine young man that this country should be proud of."

I felt very uncomfortable[4]. When I introduced him to Herbert, Herbert tried to shake his hand. Joe backed away[5]. He certainly wasn't behaving like the Joe I once knew.

1. **let go** 放手；放開
2. **awkward** [`ɒːkwərd] (a.) 笨拙的；尷尬的
3. **tightly** [`taɪtli] (adv.) 緊緊地
4. **uncomfortable** [ʌn`kʌmfərtəbəl] (a.) 不舒服的
5. **back away** 退後；退卻
6. **bow** [baʊ] (v.) 鞠躬；低（頭）
7. **bitter** [`bɪtər] (a.) 苦的；有苦味的
8. **pour** [pɔːr] (v.) 倒；注
9. **stiffly** [`stɪfli] (adv.) 僵硬地；拘謹地
10. **relieved** [rɪ`liːvd] (a.) 解脫的

Joe bowed[6] his head.

"Would you like some tea or coffee, Mr. Gargery?" Herbert asked.

"Thank you, sir," Joe said uncomfortably. "I will have whatever you are having."

Herbert suggested, "Let's have some coffee, then."

Joe did not like coffee and so he said, "Isn't coffee a bit bitter[7]?"

"Then we shall have some tea," Herbert kindly said. We all sat down to breakfast and Herbert poured[8] the tea. We spoke, very stiffly[9], to one another for a while and then Herbert left for work. I felt relieved[10] when he left and so did Joe.

"Now that[1] we are alone, sir," Joe started.

I interrupted by saying, "How can you call me sir? You are like a father to me."

Joe looked at me nervously and started talking again.

"Now that we are alone, I want to tell you that I have a message from Miss Havisham."

"From Miss Havisham?" I asked in surprise[2].

"Yes, Estella is home and will be happy if you visit."

I felt my face burn. If I had known Joe had this message for me, I would have been kinder to him.

1. **now that** 既然
2. **in surprise** 吃驚地
3. **nothing but** 只有；只不過
4. **prosper** [`prɑ:spər] (v.) 成功
5. **suit** [su:t] (v.) 適合
6. **God bless you.** 願上帝祝福你！

Joe now stood up and prepared to leave.

"You are doing well, Pip, and I wish you nothing but[3] the best. I hope you prosper[4] here in London."

"Where are you going now? Aren't you going to return for dinner?" I asked him.

"Pip, I should return home. We live different lives now. You are very comfortable living this life but it doesn't suit[5] me. I belong in the country as a blacksmith. I feel very awkward here in London. God bless you[6], Pip."

Joe put his hat on, said good-bye, and left.

Orphans in the Victorian Age

Orphans were very common during the time Dickens wrote *The Great Expectations*. Life was more dangerous then, with unsafe working conditions and primitive medical techniques.

In addition, families were very large with usually eight or more children. These factors contributed to the numbers of orphans who roamed the streets of London.

If an orphan was from a rich family, relatives or inherited money made their life easier. However, the majority of orphans were from poor families and their lives became hell.

Dickens himself had to work in a factory at a very young age to support his brothers and sisters because his father was frequently in prison.

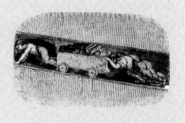

Many orphanages were built to house, feed and educate poor orphans. Unfortunately, many of the adults who managed these places were not nice people. It was not easy being an orphan then.

Most of Dickens' stories show the hard life orphans had during these times. Readers felt pity for these characters and remembered their stories well.

Chapter Four

🎧 28 # Some Terrible News

The next day I caught a coach for my hometown[1]. I felt very guilty about Joe's visit. I had not treated him like I should have. I knew that when I went to visit Miss Havisham, I should go and stay with Joe to make up for[2] his terrible time in London.

But I also knew that Joe would feel awkward. He would be worried that his dirty old house would not be good enough for me anymore. I decided to stay at the Blue Boar[3] Inn[4] in the village instead.

I knew that I should visit Joe first; however, I went to Miss Havisham's house.

"She adopted Estella and I am sure she has been helping me, too. She must like me and want me to marry Estella," I thought. I felt better every time I thought of Estella.

I arrived at the house and rang[5] the doorbell[6]. I was very surprised because a new employee[7] answered the door. It was Orlick. Joe must have[8] fired[9] him.

1. **hometown** [ˋhoʊmˋtaʊn] (n.) 家鄉；故鄉
2. **make up for** 為了彌補……
3. **boar** [bɔ:r] (n.) 公豬；野豬
4. **inn** [ɪn] (n.) 小旅館；客棧
5. **ring** [rɪ;] (v.) 按（鈴）；敲（鐘）（ring-rang-rung）
6. **doorbell** [ˋdɔ:rˋbel] (n.) 門鈴
7. **employee** [ɪmˋplɔɪi:] (n.) 受雇員；員工
8. **must have** + 過去分詞 一定已經
9. **fire** [faɪr] (v.) 解雇；開除

Orlick looked at me with scorn[1] and said, "There are changes everywhere in the world!"

I ignored[2] him and entered the house.

Miss Havisham was sitting quietly in a chair in the banquet[3] room and standing beside the fire was a woman I had never seen before.

"Miss Havisham. I heard that you wished to see me, so I came as soon as I could."

On hearing my voice, the woman by the fire turned around. It was Estella! She had grown up and become incredibly[4] beautiful. I felt as if I had not changed at all. I was still the same country boy.

---

1. **scorn** [skɔːrn] (n.)
   輕蔑；藐視
2. **ignore** [ɪg`nɔːr] (v.)
   不理會；忽視
3. **banquet** [`bæŋkwɪt] (n.)
   宴會；盛宴
4. **incredibly** [ɪn`krɛdɪbli] (adv.) 難以置信地
5. **graceful** [`greɪsfəl] (a.)
   優美的；雅緻的
6. **frighten** [`fraɪtn] (v.)
   使驚恐；使害怕

Estella looked at me and Miss Havisham asked her, "Has he changed, Estella?"

"Yes, he has changed very much." Then, Estella left the room.

Miss Havisham said, "She is graceful[5] and beautiful, isn't she?" Her next words frightened[6] me very much. She took my hand and pulled me close to her.

In my ear, she whispered, "Love her, love her, love her! If she loves you, love her. If she rejects[1] you, love her. And if she breaks your heart[2], love her."

I was so surprised that I didn't know how to reply.

"Pip! I adopted her to be loved. I raised her to be loved. I want you to love her, love her!"

Miss Havisham seemed like she had gone crazy[3].

She pointed to the door. "Go to her, Pip! She went into the garden. Go and talk to her. Walk with her," she ordered me.

I left Miss Havisham and went to find Estella. She was standing in the garden with her back to me. I awkwardly spoke to her.

1. **reject** [rɪˋdʒɛkt] (v.) 拒絕
2. **break one's heart** 傷了……的心
3. **go crazy** 失去理智
4. **further** [ˋfɜːrðər] (adv.) 更遠地；較遠地
5. **beat** [biːt] (v.) 跳動
6. **stab** [stæb] (v.) 刺入；戳
7. **shoot** [ʃuːt] (v.) 射中；射傷 (shoot-shot-shot)
8. **compassion** [kəmˋpæʃən] (n.) 憐憫；同情
9. **empty** [ˋɛmptɪ] (a.) 空洞的；無意義的
10. **sound** [saʊnd] (v.) 聽起來

She was like a fine lady in the way she walked and talked and I felt like a little boy beside her instead of the true gentleman I wanted to be. She showed no interest in me. I certainly knew that she had not thought of me like I did of her.

We walked a little further[4] through the garden and she suddenly said to me, "I have a beating[5] heart inside me which can be stabbed[6] or shot[7] but I have no heart which can feel love, compassion[8] or tenderness."

She spoke to me in a very cold voice. It was cold and empty[9] sounding[10] like the rooms in Miss Havisham's house. But when I looked into her face, I saw something familiar about her in another person I had seen. I tried to think where but I could not.

31

After my visit to Miss Havisham's house,
I left to return to London immediately. I did
not visit Joe. I knew I would not be able to talk
to Joe like I wanted to because my mind was
filled with thoughts of Estella. Miss
Havisham's words kept ringing[1] in my ears.

A few months later, I received some terrible
news. My sister died, so I returned to Joe's
house to find it filled with people from the
village. Everyone was sad. I found Joe sitting in
a chair in one corner looking very grim[2].
He was dressed in black.

I went over to him and asked, "Dear Joe,
how are you?"

He looked up and said, "Oh, Pip! It's good
to see you. I'm so glad you came. Do you
remember when she was full of energy and
youth?"

1. **keep V-ing** 繼續……
2. **grim** [grɪm] (a.)
   憂愁的；沮喪的
3. **weep** [wiːp] (v.)
   哭泣；流淚
   (weep-wept-wept)
4. **say farewell** 道別；說再見
5. **breeze** [briːz] (n.) 微風
6. **blow** [bloʊ] (v.) 吹
   (blow-blew-blown)
7. **lighten** [ˈlaɪtn] (v.)
   使光明；照亮

Then, he wept[3] in that cold empty corner of the room.

Later, Joe, I and the rest of the village went to the graveyard to bury my sister next to my mother and father and to say farewell[4] to her. Even though it was a very sad day, the birds sang in the trees and a very light breeze[5] blew[6] to lighten[7] our heavy hearts.

32

After my sister's funeral[1], I returned to London. My life continued[2] on and finally, my twenty-first birthday came. Like I had expected, Mr. Jaggers came to tell me that my yearly[3] income[4] would be much larger now. I had also expected to find out[5] who my benefactor was.

However, Mr. Jaggers didn't tell me and so I asked, "I would like to[6] know who very kindly gives me all this money."

Mr. Jaggers replied, "You will find out when your benefactor wants you to know."

I was very confused. I was absolutely sure that it was Miss Havisham and I couldn't understand why she didn't want me to know.

Even though Mr. Jaggers came with good news that day, he also had some bad news. He told me that Drummle was courting[7] Estella. I was completely taken aback[8] and left to visit Miss Havisham the next day.

1. **funeral** [ˈfjuːnərəl] (n.)
   喪葬；葬禮
2. **continue** [kənˈtɪnjuː] (v.)
   繼續；持續
3. **yearly** [ˈjɪrli] (a.)
   每年的；年度的

4. **income** [ˈɪnkʌm] (n.) 收入
5. **find out** 找出
6. **would like to** 想要
7. **court** [kɔːrt] (v.)
   求婚；示愛
8. **take aback** 使震驚

33

I arrived quite early in the day and when I entered the house, I found Miss Havisham sitting next to a fire. Estella was sitting on a stool[1] doing some knitting[2]. When I saw her, she was obviously[3] upset[4]. She threw her knitting to one side and stood up impatiently.

This bothered[5] Miss Havisham who cried, "What are you doing? Are you sick of[6] me?"

Estella answered in a dim[7] voice, "I am just tired of myself."

"Tell me the truth! I know you are tired of me!" demanded the old woman. Estella did not reply and this made Miss Havisham even angrier.

"You are so cold! You have a stone for a heart!"

1. **stool** [stuːl] (n.)
   凳子；擱腳凳
2. **knit** [nɪt] (v.) 編織
   (knit-knitted-knitted)
3. **obviously** [ˋɑːbviəsli]
   (adv.) 明顯地；顯然地
4. **upset** [ʌpˋset] (v.)
   心煩意亂的
5. **bother** [ˋbɑːðər] (v.)
   使惱怒

6. **be sick of** 對……感到厭煩
   (= be tired of)
7. **dim** [dɪm] (a.)
   模糊的，朦朧的
8. **argue** [ˋɑːrgjuː] (v.)
   爭吵；爭辯
9. **take the blame for**
   承擔……的過失
10. **snap** [snæp] (v.)
   厲聲說；怒氣沖沖地頂撞

This surprised Estella who replied, "What? You think I'm cold?"

"Well, Estella! You are," Miss Havisham told her.

Every time I had seen them together, they had been very calm. It surprised me very much to see them arguing[8].

Estella now replied, "Well, if I am cold, it's because you made me that way. You can take all the blame for[9] it."

Miss Havisham was quite upset and she said to me, "Pip! She is so proud, isn't she? Didn't I give her all the love I could?"

"Well, who taught me to be cold and hard?" Estella snapped[10]. "It is your fault."

34

"But I didn't teach you to be this way to me," the old woman said sadly. She put her arms out[1], wanting Estella to come to her.

"You taught me that love is an enemy[2]," Estella said quietly.

The two women said nothing to each other for a few moments. It seemed like the argument was over[3]. Miss Havisham sat in her chair looking very sad and Estella stood by the fire. Estella went back to her stool, sat down and picked up her knitting.

Now that everything had calmed[4] between the two, I thought that it was my best opportunity[5] to ask Estella about Drummle.

1. **put out** 伸出
2. **enemy** [ˋɛnəmi] (n.) 敵人
3. **over** [ˋouvər] (a.) 結束的；完了的
4. **calm** [kɑːm] (v.) 鎮定下來；平靜下來
5. **opportunity** [͵ɑːpərˋtuːnəti] (n.) 良機；機會 (= chance)

"Why are you spending time with Drummle? He is selfish[6], lazy, stupid and has a bad temper[7]. You deserve[8] better than that," I asked her.

She did not look at me when she replied, "Moths[9] and many ugly insects[10] fly to the light of a candle. Is the candle to blame[11]?"

"No, but you can help it," I said.

She stopped knitting and looked into the fire.

I sat down to look into her face. It was my chance to tell her how I felt. "Estella, I love you. I have always loved you since the first time I saw you," I told her. "I know that you will never love me or want to be with me but I love you anyway.

"Your words mean nothing to me. I told you that I have no heart that can feel love. I warned[12] you about this once." She was right.

---

6. **selfish** [ˋselfɪʃ] (a.) 自私的
7. **temper** [ˋtempər] (n.) 脾氣；性情
8. **deserve** [dɪˋzɜːrv] (v.) 應得；值得
9. **moth** [mɒːθ] (n.) 蛾
10. **insect** [ˋɪnsekt] (n.) 昆蟲
11. **blame** [bleɪm] (v.) 責備；指責
12. **warn** [wɔːrn] (v.) 警告；提醒

🎧35

    "I am spending time with Bentley Drummle. He will be here tonight to have dinner with us," she told me.

    I asked her, "Yes, but do you love him? Are you going to marry him?"

    I greatly feared[1] Estella's answer. I knew that if she married Drummle she would regret[2] it for the rest[3] of her life.

1. **fear** [fɪr] (v.) 害怕；懼怕
2. **regret** [rɪˋgrɛt] (v.) 懊悔；遺憾
3. **rest** [rɛst] (n.) 剩餘的部分；其餘
4. **shatter** [ˋʃætɚ] (v.) 粉碎
5. **beg** [bɛg] (v.) 懇求；請求
6. **revenge** [rɪˋvɛndʒ] (n.) 報仇；復仇

"I told you before that I cannot love. But I will marry him," she said.

I felt my life had just been shattered[4] into a thousand pieces.

"Estella, please don't marry him," I begged[5] her. "Miss Havisham only taught you that love is the enemy because her own heart was broken. She only wanted revenge[6]. You will be so unhappy with Drummle."

"I will marry him whether you like it or not. It has nothing to do with[7] you or my adoptive mother[8]. It is my decision and my mistake to make," Estella said.

I felt very angry and I shouted, "Drummle is an idiot. He doesn't deserve you."

Estella took my hand and said, "We will never understand each other but at least let's try to be friends." I took her hand and pressed[9] my lips to it. My tears rolled down my cheeks and onto[10] her beautiful soft, white skin.

---

7. **have nothing to do with**
   與……無關
8. **adoptive mother** 養母

9. **press** [pres] (v.) 緊壓
10. **onto** [ˋɑːntu] (prep.)
    到……之上

A Fill in the blanks with character's names according to the story.

❶ _____ stayed at the Blue Boar Inn when he went to visit _____.

❷ Pip hoped that _____ wanted him to marry _____.

❸ _____ said that _____ had changed very much.

❹ _____ was now working at Miss Havisham's house.

❺ Miss Havisham wanted _____ to love _____.

❻ _____ wept when _____'s sister died.

B Correct and Rewrite the sentences.

As he was promised, Herbert told me Miss Havisham.
⇨ As he promised, Herbert told me *about* Miss Havisham.

❶ He asked a friend pretending fall in love with her.

⇨ _____

❷ He taught me what to dress and what to behave at parties.

⇨ _____

❸ Dinner was served by the woman whose looked about forty years old.

⇨ _____

C Rearrange the sentences in chronological order.

❶ Pip received a letter from Biddy.

❷ Herbert told Pip about Miss Havisham.

❸ Pip arrived at Mr. Jaggers' office in London.

❹ Joe visited Pip in London.

❺ The clerk took Pip to Mr. Pocket's house.

_____ ⇨ _____ ⇨ _____ ⇨ _____ ⇨ _____

D Fill in the blanks with the given words.

come   reply   give   not tell   return   expect

After my sister's funeral, I ❶ _____ to London. My life continued on and finally, my twenty-first birthday came. Like I ❷ _____, Mr. Jaggers ❸ _____ to tell me that my yearly income would be much larger now. I had also expected to find out who my benefactor was. However, Mr. Jaggers ❹ _____ me and so I asked, "I would like to know who very kindly ❺ _____ me all this money." Mr. Jaggers ❻ _____, "You will find out when your benefactor wants you to know."

Chapter Five

🎧 36 My Benefactor

Time seemed to go by very quickly. Before I knew it, I was twenty-three years old. I was not living with Herbert's father anymore. Instead, Herbert and I had moved into a place called Garden Court which was by the river.

Over the past few days there had been some terrible weather in London. It had rained constantly[1] and because of this, I had stayed indoors[2] the whole time. I was feeling very depressed. Herbert was in France on business and I missed[3] his cheerfulness[4].

---

1. **constantly** [`kɑ:nstəntli] (adv.) 不斷地；時常地
2. **indoors** [`ɪn`dɔ:rz] (adv.) 在室內；在屋裡
3. **miss** [mɪs] (v.) 惦記；想念
4. **cheerfulness** [`tʃɪrfəlnəs] (n.) 爽朗
5. **footstep** [`fʊt͵step] (n.) 腳步；步伐
6. **hallway** [`hɔ:l͵weɪ] (n.) 門廳

That evening, I was in my room doing some reading.

Suddenly I heard the sound of footsteps[5]. I took my lamp out into the hallway[6] and called out, "Is anyone there?"

"Yes," said a voice.

"Who are you looking for?" I asked.

The voice said, "Mr. Pip."

"I am Mr. Pip," I replied.

A man slowly walked up the stairs. He was about sixty years old and he was dressed like a seaman[1].

"What do you want?" I asked him.

"I will tell you," he said.

We went into my room and he took off his coat. He put out both his hands for me to take. Since I did not recognize[2] him, I was worried that he was crazy.

"I have waited so long for this day. Please give me a moment," he said.

He sat down and looked around nervously[3].

"Is there anyone with you tonight?" he asked.

"Excuse me," I said. "But you are a stranger here. You have no right to ask that."

The man laughed and said, "You are quite bold. I am glad you grew up to be bold[4]."

Just then, I recognized the man. He was the man I had met in the graveyard many years ago. He was the escaped prisoner! I didn't know what to say. He put his hands out again and not knowing what to do, I put my hands in his.

---

1. **seaman** [ˋsiːmən] (n.)
   水手；海員
2. **recognize** [ˋrekəgnaɪz]
   (v.) 認出；指出

3. **nervously** [ˋnɜːrvəsli]
   (adv.) 提心吊膽地
4. **bold** [boʊld] (a.)
   大膽的；英勇的

38

He continued, "I have always been grateful[1] for how you helped me that day in the graveyard."

I pulled away from[2] him.

"I don't need you to thank me for that. I just hope that you are a changed man," I said harshly[3] to him.

He looked hurt, so I said more kindly, "You must stay and have a drink before you go. You are tired and wet."

I gave him something warm to drink and then he told me about what had happened to him. He escaped from the prison one more time and made his way to[4] Australia. There, he became a sheep farmer[5] and made a lot of money[6].

1. **grateful** [ˋgreɪtfəl] (a.)
   感激的；感謝的
2. **pull away from**
   把……推開
3. **harshly** [ˋhɑːrʃli] (adv.)
   厲聲地
4. **make one's way to**
   成功前往……
5. **sheep farmer**
   牧羊農場主人
6. **make money** 賺錢
7. **stutter** [ˋstʌtər] (v.)
   結結巴巴地說話
8. **by any chance**
   萬一；也許
9. **guardian** [ˋgɑːrdiən] (n.)
   監護人
10. **turn** [tɜːrn] (v.)
    變成

"I see you have done well in life, too," he said. "Tell me your story."

"Well, I have a benefactor," I stuttered[7].

"Really! Does your yearly income begin with the number five by any chance[8]?" he asked me.

I was very surprised because my income was five hundred pounds.

"How could he know that?" I thought.

Then he asked me, "You had a guardian[9] before you turned[10] twenty one, didn't you? His name begins with a J, doesn't it? Is his name Jaggers?"

39

I was horrified[1]. I knew the truth now. This man was my benefactor and not Miss Havisham like I first thought. The prisoner saw how shocked[2] I was.

"Yes, Pip! I made you a gentleman. After what you did for me, I promised myself that I would work hard so that you could live well," he said.

I stepped back[3] from him. I felt terrible that such a man had paid for[4] the life I had been living. I was quite[5] depressed[6].

My great expectations[7] were dust[8]. Miss Havisham wasn't my benefactor. I had hoped so much that Miss Havisham wanted me to marry Estella. It was all a dream!

Then, I thought of Joe. "Poor Joe! I deserted[9] wonderful, kind-hearted[10] Joe for a criminal[11]."

The man took my hands again and as he did so, I felt my heart pound[12] in my chest.

1. **horrify** [ˈhɔːrəfaɪ] (v.) 使恐懼；使驚恐
2. **shocked** [ʃɑːkt] (a.) 震驚的
3. **step back** 往後退 (step-stepped-stepped)
4. **pay for** 付出代價
5. **quite** [kwaɪt] (adv.) 相當地
6. **depressed** [dɪˈprest] (a.) 沮喪的；消沉的
7. **expectation** [ˌekspekˈteɪʃən] (n.) 預期；期望

"I must sleep somewhere tonight. I have been at sea for months and months," he told me.

Even though I did not want the man to stay in my house, I allowed him to sleep in Herbert's room.

8. **dust** [dʌst] (n.) 塵土；灰塵
9. **desert** [dɪˋzɜːrt] (v.)
   遺棄；離棄
10. **kind-hearted**
    [ˋkaɪndˋhɑːrtɪd] (a.)
    仁慈的；好心的
11. **criminal** [ˋkrɪmɪnəl] (n.)
    罪犯
12. **pound** [paʊnd] (v.)
    （心）劇跳

🎧 40

The next morning, we ate breakfast together and he told me that his name was Abel Magwitch. He ate breakfast quickly and as soon as he had finished[1], he stood up and put a wallet[2] on the table. It was full of money.

1. **finish** [`fɪnɪʃ] (v.)
   結束；吃完
2. **wallet** [`wɑːlɪt] (n.)
   皮夾；錢包
3. **for good** 永久地
4. **appearance** [ə`pɪrəns]
   (n.) 外貌；外觀

5. **hang** [hæ;] (v.) 絞死；吊死
6. **hold** [hould] (v.)
   持著；托著
7. **swear** [swer] (v.)
   發誓；宣誓
   (swear-swore-sworn)

"It's for you, Pip," he said. "I want you to buy the best of everything and be a real gentleman."

"No," I shouted. "I don't want your money. It's not mine. All I want to know is if the police are looking for you. I hope you won't be staying long. You're only visiting for a short while, aren't you?"

"No. I will be in England for good[3]," he said. "I can change my appearance[4] but if the police catch me, they will hang[5] me. You have to find a place for me to live."

I didn't know what to do, so Magwitch hid in my room. A few days later, Herbert came back from France. I had to tell him.

Magwitch made Herbert hold[6] a Bible and said, "Swear[7] you won't tell anyone that you saw me." I felt awful. After all of Herbert's kindness to me, I didn't want to force him to keep this secret.

Later that day when I was alone with Herbert, he said, "He can't stay here. He has to leave England and he won't go without you."

Herbert was right. I would never be free if Magwitch stayed in England. I decided never to take any money but after he had given so much to me, I hated the thought of the police catching him.

He continued to stay in our apartment and only went out at night for some fresh air.

Not long after, the guard[1] warned me that he had seen a stranger outside of our place. The man had a long scar, and wore old, torn[2] clothes. The guard said he seemed to be looking up at our windows.

"He must be after[3] Magwitch," I thought.

1. **guard** [gɑːrd] (n.)
   守衛；警衛
2. **torn** [tɔːrn] (a.)
   破的；被撕扯的
3. **be after** 跟蹤；追蹤
4. **used to** + 原形動詞／**be** 動詞
   曾經是……

The next morning, I asked, "Do you know a man with a long scar on his face? The guard said a man with a scar has been watching our place."

"I know who he is. His name is Compeyson. He used to[4] be a gentleman but he was also a thief."

He continued, "I met him a long time ago and I became his partner. Together, we planned to cheat[1] people out of money in the horse races[2]. He had the ideas and I did the dirty work[3]. We were eventually[4] caught and he, looking like a gentleman, said I was the guilty one. He was sent to prison for only seven years whereas[5] I got fourteen years. I promised to get revenge one day."

I looked at Magwitch. I could see the anger in his eyes.

"Eventually, we both escaped from the prison on the same night. We found each other in a field and fought. That was around the time when you and I met in the graveyard," he said.

There was silence between us for a few moments and then he said, "I heard you know Miss Havisham. Is that right?"

"Yes," I answered.

"Then you would be interested to know that Compeyson was a friend of Miss Havisham's half-brother. He was the man who pretended to love her and then deserted her on her wedding day," Magwitch informed[6] me.

The pieces of this strange puzzle[7] were starting to fit[8] together.

---

1. **cheat** [tʃiːt] (v.) 欺騙；詐取
2. **horse race** 賽馬
3. **dirty work** 卑鄙勾當；不法行為
4. **eventually** [ɪˋventʃuəlɪ] (adv.) 最後；終於
5. **whereas** [werˋæz] (conj.) 反之；卻；而
6. **inform** [ɪnˋfɔːrm] (v.) 告知；報告
7. **puzzle** [ˋpʌzəl] (n.) 謎；難以理解之事
8. **fit** [fɪt] (v.) 合；使適合

Herbert and I had to get Magwitch away from[1] Compeyson. In a week, we moved him to another place right on the river. He stayed at Herbert's girlfriend's house at Mill Pond Bank.

Magwitch and I planned to catch a steam boat[2] to leave England. I didn't know exactly when the safest time would be to get Magwitch onto the boat so I rowed[3] past[4] the house every evening. I was waiting for a sign[5] from Herbert.

One day, I received a message from Mr. Jaggers. He wanted me to join him for dinner. I went and heard that there was a message from Miss Havisham.

1. **get away form** 從⋯⋯逃脫
2. **steam boat** 汽船
3. **row** [rou] (v.) 划船
4. **past** [pæst] (prep.) 經過;通過
5. **sign** [saɪn] (n.) 暗號

"She would like you to visit her. She also wants you to know that Estella and Drummle are married," Mr. Jaggers told me.

I was completely taken by surprise[6]. I had forgotten all about Estella since the arrival of Magwitch.

As I sat there, thinking about Estella and Drummle, the housekeeper[7] brought out[8] the dinner. Each time she served a dish, I kept thinking to myself, "Who does she remind me of [9]?"

Then, I realized that she looked just like Estella. Could she be Estella's real mother? For the rest of the evening, I could think of nothing else.

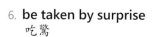

6. **be taken by surprise** 吃驚
7. **housekeeper** 管家
8. **bring out** 拿出；取出
9. **remind A of** 使 A 想起……

The next morning, I set out[1] to visit Miss Havisham. When I arrived, the house was in terrible condition but the worst thing was that Estella was gone. I saw Miss Havisham sitting in the banquet room. She looked so lonely.

"Who is it?" she asked.

"It is Pip," I answered.

I sat down next to her. She started to speak.

"My heart is not made of[2] stone. If I could change Estella, I would. I regret raising[3] her to be so cold. If you can forgive me, please do so," she begged.

"I have already forgiven you," I said.

"I have caused[4] hurt to others too, you know."

Then I asked her, "Whose child is Estella?"

1. **set out** 啟程
2. **be make of** 以……製成的
3. **raise** [reɪz] (v.) 養育；扶養
4. **cause** [kɔːz] (v.) 導致；致使
5. **be accused of** 被控告……
6. **murder** [ˋmɜːrdər] (n.) 謀殺；謀殺罪
7. **take a last look at** 看……最後一眼
8. **flame** [fleɪm] (n.) 火焰；火舌
9. **wrap** [ræp] (v.) 包覆；裹
10. **scream** [skriːm] (v.) 尖叫
11. **burn** [bɜːrn] (v.) 燒傷；灼傷
12. **unbearable** [ʌnˋberəbəl] (a.) 無法忍受的；難以忍受的

Miss Havisham shook her head.

"Mr. Jaggers brought her to you, didn't he?"

"Yes, when she was about two or three. Her real mother was accused of[5] murder[6]. Jaggers was her lawyer. He didn't tell me anything else about her mother."

Evening came and it was time for me to leave. In the courtyard, I turned to take a last look at[7] the old house. Flames[8] were coming out of the window of the banquet room!

I ran into the house. Miss Havisham's old dress had caught on fire! The fire continued and I pulled the table cloth off the table and wrapped[9] her in it. She screamed[10] in pain.

At last the fire was out and I looked at my hands. They had also been burned[11] by the fire. The burns were unbearable[12]. A doctor came to take care of Miss Havisham and me. I left soon after.

Ships for Australia

Laws in eighteenth century England were much stricter than they are today. People were hanged not only for murder, but also for stealing! People were thrown into prison for breaking promises of marriage or for borrowing more money than they could pay back. Under these strict laws, English prisons became very crowded. This became a problem.

At the time, England had many colonies around the world. One colony, Australia, had a lot of land and hardly any people. The English government decided that by shipping prisoners to Australia, they could solve two problems.

Firstly the criminals leave England and the prisons would be emptied. Secondly, Australia would get the manpower it needed to become a productive colony. The prisoners who were transported to Australia could eventually become free men and women if they worked hard.

This is how Magwitch, Pip's benefactor, could change from being a wretched prisoner to a rich sheep farmer. However, if these former prisoners ever returned to England, they would be put back in jail or even executed.

Chapter Six

 Another New Beginning

The fire had badly burned my left arm all the way[1] to the shoulder. My right arm was not so bad. Herbert had to change my bandages[2] for me every day.

One day, as he helped me, he said, "I had an interesting conversation with Magwitch the other day. He said that he was married once. People say his wife, out of jealousy[3], murdered another woman."

I was very excited by this.

---

1. **all the way to** 一直到……
2. **bandage** [`bændɪdʒ] (n.) 繃帶
3. **out of jealousy** 出自妒忌

"Jaggers took her case[4]. No one saw the crime. She didn't have to go to jail[5]," added Herbert.

"When?" I asked him.

"It was about the time he met you. He also had a child about the same age as you in the graveyard and you reminded him of his lost child. That's why he has helped you all this time."

"Herbert! I think Estella is Magwitch's lost child," I cried. "I must find out for sure[6]."

4. **case** [keɪs] (n.) 案件；訴訟
5. **jail** [dʒeɪl] (n.) 監獄
6. **for sure** 確切地

46

The next day, I went to see Mr. Jaggers.

"You took the child to Miss Havisham, didn't you? I know who her mother is. She is the housekeeper here," I told him.

"Really?" he replied. Then, I told him Miss Havisham's and Magwitch's stories.

"It is true. I wanted to help a poor child who had no future. There are so many of them in this world," he said.

"Her father was in and out of jail and her mother was accused[1] of murder. I had to help the poor child. I gave the child a good home and her mother a job. It is our secret to keep, Pip."

1. **accuse** [ə`kjuːz] (v.) 控告
2. **fever** [`fiːvər] (n.) 發燒
3. **swollen** [`swoulən] (a.) 腫脹的；浮腫的
4. **incredibly** [ɪn`kredəbli] (adv.) 難以置信地；極為
5. **get onto** 登上……
6. **steamer** [`stiːmər] (n.) 汽船；輪船

The next day, when I woke up, I had a
fever[2]. My arm was very swollen[3] and red.
It was incredibly[4] painful.

I slept for two days and Herbert changed
my bandages every few hours. I had to be well
enough to get onto[5] the steam boat with
Magwitch on Wednesday. Startop agreed to
help us row the boat to the steamer[6].

47

Wednesday came and I put on a heavy coat and took one bag. We went down to the river to Mill Pond Bank and Magwitch was waiting for us.

He got into the boat and said, "Thank you for doing this. It will be wonderful to enjoy freedom again."

"Soon, you will be able to enjoy that freedom," I said.

We rowed for a long time down the river. We waited and at about one thirty, we finally saw the smoke of the steamer. I felt very sad as I said good-bye to Herbert.

The steamer came very close and just as we were about to[1] call out to the captain[2], another boat appeared. There were three men in it and one of them was a policeman.

1. **be about to** 即將……
2. **captain** [`kæptɪn] (n.)
   船長;艦長
3. **arrest** [ə`rest] (v.)
   逮捕
4. **yell out** 大聲地叫出

5. **disappear** [ˌdɪsə`pɪr] (v.)
   消失
6. **drag into** 拖進去……
   (drag-dragged-dragged)
7. **handcuff** [`hændkʌf] (v.)
   給……戴上手銬

"You have the escaped prisoner, Abel Magwitch, in your boat. Arrest[3] him," he yelled out[4].

The boat hit ours. Then, I could see Compeyson in the other boat. Magwitch jumped at him and the two men fell into the river. They fought in the water and then both disappeared[5].

A few moments later, I saw Magwitch swimming away but the policeman caught him. He dragged him into[6] the boat and handcuffed[7] him.

48

Magwitch was badly hurt. He had broken one of his ribs[1] which had injured[2] a lung[3]. Compeyson was found dead. He had drowned[4].

Magwitch was taken back to prison and I went to see him there. He became very sick. As he had been so good to me, I could not desert him like I had deserted Joe.

Later, at his court trial[5], he was found guilty[6] of murdering Compeyson. The police said that he did not drown. Now Magwitch had to spend the rest of his life in jail.

One morning, he asked me, "Pip, are you always the first one to arrive at the prison?"

"Yes," I told him. "Our time together is too precious[7] to waste[8]."

"Thank you for being so faithful[9] to me." Magwitch then groaned[10] in pain[11]. He put his head on his pillow[12].

1. **rib** [rɪb] (n.) 肋骨
2. **injure** [ˈɪndʒər] (v.) 傷害；損害
3. **lung** [lʌŋ] (n.) 肺；肺臟
4. **drown** [draʊn] (v.) 溺死

5. **trial** [ˈtraɪəl] (n.) 審問；審判
6. **be found guilty** 被判定有罪

"Magwitch, can you hear me?" I asked.
He squeezed[13] my hand.

I said, "I know you had a child who you loved but lost. I know her and I love her. She is a beautiful, fine lady."

Magwitch took my hand and pressed it to his lips. Then, quietly, his head dropped onto his chest. It was over. His face looked peaceful as he died that day.

7. **precious** [ˋprɛʃəs] (a.)
貴重的；珍貴的

8. **waste** [weɪst] (v.)
浪費；濫用

9. **faithful** [ˋfeɪθfl] (a.)
忠實的；忠貞的

10. **groan** [groʊn] (v.) 呻吟

11. **in pain** 在痛苦中

12. **pillow** [ˋpɪloʊ] (n.) 枕頭

13. **squeeze** [skwiːz] (v.)
擠；壓；搾

117

🎧 49

After Magwitch died, I became very sick. My whole body ached[1] and I couldn't move. During that time, two men came to collect[2] some money I owed[3]. I didn't have any so they said, "Then you must come with us."

I said in a small voice, "I would if I could. But I might die on the way[4]." I could not hear their reply.

For the next few days, I have no memory of what happened. I dreamed of Joe and I thought I saw him sitting on a chair in the room. It was a strange dream.

One day, I awoke[5] to see Joe reading one of my books.

"Water! I need some water!" I said in a weak voice. A hand gave me a glass of water.

"Joe, is it really you?" I asked.

"Of course, it is," he said.

"Joe, I don't deserve to be treated so well after I treated you so badly.

1. **ache** [eɪk] (v.) 疼痛
2. **collect** [kəˋlɛkt] (v.) 收款；收帳
3. **owe** [oʊ] (v.) 欠
4. **on the way** 在途中
5. **awake** [əˋweɪk] (v.) 醒來
6. **what about . . .?** ……怎麼樣？

"We're old friends, Pip. I would do anything for you," he said kindly.

"Have you been here the whole time?" I asked.

"Almost," he answered.

"We heard that you were sick so Biddy told me to come."

"What about[6] Miss Havisham?" I asked.

"She died about a week after you became sick," he said.

50

With Joe taking wonderful care of me, I quickly recovered[1]. He even took me into the country to get some fresh air. For a long time, I had not been able to walk. But there in the country I tried to walk a few steps.

I said, "It won't be long until I am walking again."

Joe replied, "Just do it slowly, alright?"

A few days later, Joe asked me, "Are you feeling stronger now?"

"Yes, every day I am becoming stronger," I said.

But the next morning when I woke up, Joe had left. He left me a note that said I was well enough to live my life as a gentleman again, and he did not want to be a bother[2] to me. With a note was a receipt[3] for my bills[4]. He had paid everything for me.

1. **recover** [rɪˋkʌvər] (v.)
   恢復健康
2. **bother** [ˋbɑːðər] (n.)
   煩擾；麻煩
3. **receipt** [rɪˋsiːt] (n.) 收據
4. **bill** [bɪl] (n.) 帳單
5. **workroom** [ˋwɜːrkrʊm] (n.)
   工作室；工場
6. **spoil** [spɔɪl] (v.)
   搞砸；破壞

I had to go to his home and thank him. I had also thought about Biddy a lot. I planned to ask her to marry me, and I hoped that she would be able to see that I had changed.

Three days later, I went to visit Joe. I went into his workroom[5] but everything was closed. I went and looked through the windows of the house. There were flowers everywhere. I went inside and found Joe sitting beside Biddy. They were dressed in their best clothes.

Biddy saw me and cried, "Pip! Today is our wedding day." I was very happy I had not told Joe about my plans for Biddy. They were both so excited to see me.

I could not spoil[6] their happiness.

51

"Biddy, you have the best husband in the world and Joe, you have the best wife in the world," I congratulated them.

Then I said, "I will leave England today. I owe you my life and I am going to repay[1] all of the money you used to pay my bills. I wish you all the best. I hope you have a child and please tell him that I love you both. I know he will be a better man than I."

I left them and went to join Herbert's company. I worked hard and I became a partner[2]. Herbert eventually married Clara and we all lived very happily together.

Eleven years later, I returned to visit Joe and Biddy. I arrived at their home and looked in through the window. Biddy was beside the fire doing some knitting and Joe was smoking his pipe.

1. **repay** [rɪˋpeɪ] (v.)
   償還；報答
   (repay-repaid-repaid)

2. **partner** [ˋpɑːrtnər] (n.)
   合夥；共同出資者
3. **name after** 以⋯⋯為名

I saw a small boy sitting on one of the kitchen chairs. They were so happy to see me.

"This is our son, Pip," they told me. "We named him after[3] you."

I stayed with them for a few days and one evening, Biddy asked, "Pip, why haven't you ever married?"

"Well, I guess I am so comfortable living with Herbert and Clara," I answered.

Then Biddy asked, "Do you think of her often?"

Biddy knew my heart very well but I just said, "That part of my life is over."

52

I discovered that Estella's marriage had ended. She had been very unhappy and Drummle was eventually killed by a horse he had been beating.

I walked over to visit Miss Havisham's old house. Everything was gone except for[1] the old rocks for the garden wall.
A gate was still there and I pushed it. I walked around the old garden and thought of the many times I had been there before. Suddenly, in the distance, I saw someone.

"Estella!" I cried. She came and I saw that she had changed.

"I have changed a lot, haven't I?" she asked. She had a new beauty that was filled with warmth and softness[2]. We found a bench and sat down.

"We met in this same place a long time ago. Seems strange, doesn't it?" I said.

1. **except for** 除了……以外
2. **softness** [ˋsɒːftnəs] (n.) 柔和；柔軟
3. **little by little** 逐漸地
4. **abroad** [əˋbrɒːd] (adv.) 海外
5. **throw away** 扔掉；拋棄
6. **valuable** [ˋvæljuəbl] (a.) 珍貴的；有價值的

124

"I feel sorry for this old place. I've had to sell everything little by little[3]. Are you still living abroad[4]?" she asked.

"Yes, I am."

"And you are very successful?" she asked again.

"Yes, and I work very hard," I replied.

"I often think about what I threw away[5] with you. But I am a much better person now. I understand what is valuable[6] in life. Please tell me I have not lost you as a friend," she said.

"You have always had a special place in my heart," I told her. Estella smiled and I took her hand in mine. We left that place together but we never left each other again.

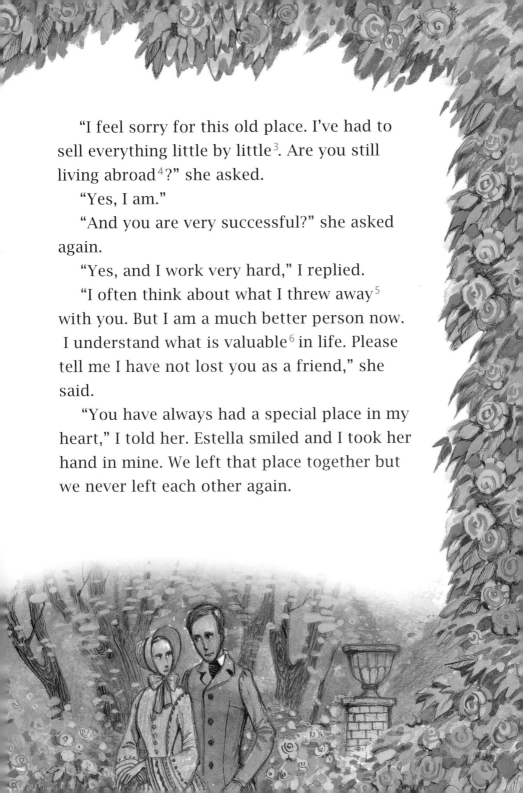

A Match the word with its meaning.

① recognize •   • ⓐ To speak in a nervous manner.

② stutter •   • ⓑ To tell someone of danger.

③ horrified •   • ⓒ To say someone is guilty of something.

④ desert •   • ⓓ To leave or abandon someone or something.

⑤ warn •   • ⓔ To remember someone's face or voice.

⑥ accuse •   • ⓕ To be extremely shocked.

B Correct and Rewrite the sentences.

Pip's whole *right* arm was badly burned to his shoulder.
⇨ Pip's whole *left* arm was badly burned to his shoulder.

① The police caught Magwitch as he was leaving the house at Mill Pond Bank.

⇨ _____

② Magwitch was found drowned in the river.

⇨ _____

③ Joe came and took care of Pip for one day.

⇨ _____

C Choose the correct answer.

1 How did Magwitch make all his money?

    (a) He won it from gambling.

    (b) He stole it from wealthy people.

    (c) He became a sheep farmer in Australia.

2 How did Pip plan to help Magwitch?

    (a) He was going to let Magwitch live with him.

    (b) He was going to help Magwitch escape from England.

    (c) He planned to ask the police to pardon him.

D Fill in the blanks with the given words.

| abandon (x 2)   damage   kill   drown   guilty |

Magwitch was badly hurt. Compeyson had broken one of his ribs which then **1** _____ a lung. Compeyson was found dead. He had **2** _____. Magwitch was taken back to prison and I went to see him there. He became very sick and as he had been so good to me and I could not **3** _____ him like I **4** _____ Joe. Later, in his court trial, he was found **5** _____ of **6** _____ Compeyson.

Guide to Listening Comprehension

 When listening to the story, use some of the techniques shown below. If you take time to study some phonetic characteristics of English, listening will be easier.

Get in the flow of English.

English creates a rhythm formed by combinations of strong and weak stress intonations. Each word has its particular stress that combines with other words to form the overall pattern of stress or rhythm in a particular sentence.

When you are speaking and listening to English, it is essential to get in the flow of the rhythm of English. It takes a lot of practice to get used to such a rhythm. So, you need to start by identifying the stressed syllable in a word.

Listen for the strongly stressed words and phrases.

In English, key words and phrases that are essential to the meaning of a sentence are stressed louder. Therefore, pay attention to the words stressed with a higher pitch. When listening to an English recording for the first time, what matters most is to listen for a general understanding of what you hear. Do not to try to hear every single word. Most of the unstressed words are articles or auxiliary verbs, which don't play an important role in the general context. At this level, you can ignore them.

Pay attention to liaisons.

In reading English, words are written with a space between them. There isn't such an obvious guide when it comes to listening to English. In oral English, there are many cases when the sounds of words are linked with adjacent words.

For instance, let's think about the phrase "take off," which can be used in "take off your clothes." "Take off your clothes" doesn't sound like [teək ɔ:f] with each of the words completely and clearly separated from the others. Instead, it sounds as if almost all the words in context are slurred together, [teəkɔ:f], for a more natural sound.

Shadow the voice of the native speaker.

Finally, you need to mimic the voice of the native speaker. Once you are sure you know how to pronounce all the words in a sentence, try to repeat them like an echo. Listen to the book again, but this time you should try a fun exercise while listening to the English.

This exercise is called "shadowing." The word "shadow" means a dark shade that is formed on a surface. When used as a verb, the word refers to the action of following someone or something like a shadow. In this exercise, pretend you are a parrot and try to shadow the voice of the native speaker.

Try to mimic the reader's voice by speaking at the same speed, with the same strong and weak stresses on words, and pausing or stopping at the same points.

Experts have already proven this technique to be effective. If you practice this shadowing exercise, your English speaking and listening skills will improve by leaps and bounds. While shadowing the native speaker, don't forget to pay attention to the meaning of each phrase and sentence.

Step 1 Listen to what you want to shadow many times. Start out by just trying to shadow a few words or a sentence.

 Step 2 Mimic the CD out loud. You can shadow everything the speaker says as if you are singing a round, or you also can speak simultaneously with the recorded voice of the native speaker.

 Step 3 As you practice more, try to shadow more. For instance, shadow a whole sentence or paragraph instead of just a few words.

以下為《孤星血淚》各章節的前半部。一開始若能聽清楚發音，之後就沒有聽力的負擔。首先，請聽過摘錄的章節，之後再反覆聆聽括內單字的發音，並仔細閱讀各種發音的說明。

以下都是以英語的典型發音為基礎，所做的簡易說明，即使這裡未提到的發音，也可以配合 CD 反覆聆聽，如此一來聽力必能更上層樓。

Chapter One page 12–13 🎧53

My story begins when I was seven years old. I was in the graveyard of the church that was very close to my home. Both of my parents (❶) ( ) ( ). Suddenly (❷) ( ) ( ) because I felt afraid and the noise of my sobs filled the graveyard.

"Who is making that awful noise?" said a low voice. A terrible looking man (❸) ( ) ( ).

"Don't move or I'll cut your throat," he said. He was dirty and was wearing leg irons. He (❹) ( ) ( ) from the local prison!

He grabbed me and I cried, "Please don't kill me!"

What's your name? Quickly!" he demanded.

"Pip," I said.

❶ were buried there: buried 和 there 連在一起發音時，buried 的 -ed 會迅速略過，幾乎聽不出其發音。

❷ I started crying: started 的發音為 [staɪrtɪd]，-rt 一起發音時，[t] 音會放在不同的音節上，而 [d] 音會迅速略過，聽不出其發音。

❸ came toward me: toward 的發音為 [təˋwɔɪrd]，與 me 合在一起發音時，[d] 音會迅速略過，不發出來。toward 的重音在第二音節，常會聽不清楚第一個音節而無法判別聽見的字為何，需依上下文來判斷。

❹ must have escaped: 在會話中，have 的 [h] 音會消失，聽起來就像 ave 的發音。[h] 音在 he、him、his、her 中，或是 have、had 中的發音在會話中常會消失不見。而 escaped 的 -ed 發 [t] 音，與前面的字連在一起發音時，[t] 音會迅速略過而聽不見其發音，需依據上下文來判斷時態。

"Where (❶) ( ) home?" he asked. I pointed to the nearby village.

He then turned me (❷) ( ) to empty my pockets. I only (❸) ( ) ( ) ( ) bread and he quickly picked it up and devoured it.

"Where are your parents?" he asked. I pointed to the gravestones in the churchyard.

"They are in the ground over there sir," I replied.

"So who do you live with?"

"My sister, sir. Wife of Joe Gargery, the blacksmith, sir," I told him.

"Blacksmith, eh? You know (❹) ( ) ( ) ( )?"

"Yes, sir," I said.

"Then you bring me a file and some food and then I won't kill you," he said.

I agreed and then he let me go.

(❺) ( ) ( ) ( ) he said again, "You bring me the file and food tonight, you hear. And don't tell anyone you saw me. If you do, I'll (❻) ( ) ( ) ( ) your heart and liver out."

❶ **is your:** is 的 [z] 音會與 your 的 [jə] 音形成連音 [dʒu]。

❷ **upside down:** upside 的 [d] 音與 down 與 [d] 音連在一起發音時，只發一次的 [d] 音。

❸ **had a piece of:** had 和 a 連在一起發音時，會形成連音 hada。而 a piece of 中，piece 的 [s] 音會與 of 的 o 連在一起發音，形成連音 [sə]，而 of 的 [v] 音也會迅速略過，不發出來。

❹ **what a file is:** what 與 a 一起發音時，what 的 [t] 音會與 a 產生連音，而此連音是介於 ta 和 da 之間的音。

❺ **just before I left:** just 和 before 連在一起發音時，just 的 [t] 音不會發出來。而 before 的重音在第二音節，be- 的音會聽不清楚，所以必須依據上下文來判斷正確文字。

❻ **find you and tear:** find 的 d 音和後面的 you 形成連音 [dʒu]，與 meet you 的例子相同，meet 的 t 音和 you 形成連音 [tʃu]。and 與 tear 連在一起發音時，and 的 [d] 音會省略不發。

3 Listening Comprehension

🎧 55 **A** Listen to the CD and fill in the blanks.

1. One night, a _____ _____ Pip in his home at Garden Court.

2. Pip dreamed that Joe was _____ _____ _____ him.

3. Estella told Pip that she _____ _____ _____ marry Drummle.

4. Magwitch died _____ _____ _____ in prison.

5. When Pip visited Estella, she and Miss Havisham _____ _____.

🎧 56 **B** Listen to the CD. Write down the sentences and names.

Mr. Jaggers   Pip   Miss Havisham   Magwitch   Herbert

1. .... ⇨ _____

2. .... ⇨ _____

3. .... ⇨ _____

4. .... ⇨ _____

5. .... ⇨ _____

🎧 57 **C** Listen to the CD, write down the sentences and choose the correct answer.

❶ _____?

(a) She is his niece.

(b) She is his daughter.

(c) She is his friend's daughter.

❷ _____?

(a) Because he felt sorry for him.

(b) Because Pip reminded him of his lost child.

(c) Because he wanted Pip to marry Estella.

🎧 58 **D** Listen to the CD and write down the sentences. Rearrange the sentences in chronological order.

1 ....

2 ....

3 ....

4 ....

5 ....

_____ ⇨ _____ ⇨ _____ ⇨ _____ ⇨ _____

　　查爾斯‧狄更斯（Charles Dickens,1812–1870）被公認為維多利亞時期最偉大的英國小說家。他的作品被歸納出具有批判社會邪惡、不公與偽善的特色。

　　查爾斯‧狄更斯 1812 年 2 月 7 日生於蘭波特。因出生貧寒，幼年未能接受正規學校教育。12 歲時，他開始在工廠工作，週薪 6 先令。

　　19 世紀早期，英國資本主義興起，替英國大都市帶來榮景。然而，資本主義也有黑暗面。童工猖獗，勞動階級的人們飽受貧窮之苦。脫胎自對社會正義的自身苦痛經驗，狄更斯具有洞見，並開始著作短篇故事教育自身。他相信對自我教育的追求能帶領他脫離貧苦。

　　狄更斯最廣為人知的作品包括《孤星血淚》（*Great Expectations*）和《孤雛淚》（*Oliver Twist*）。因對勞動階級的日常生活刻畫鮮明，他的小說受高度重視。他親身經歷並深知那些悲喜感受，筆下美麗幽默的描繪，也檢視了不公與社會矛盾的狀況。

　　狄更斯雖時常被批評，指他刻意迎合讀者的多愁善感與愛好浮誇的閱讀品味，但他被尊為偉大英國小說家的原因，如同莎士比亞（Shakespeare），在於其為角色注入的豐富人性與幽默感，展現出真實人類的過錯、堅毅與生命力。

　　1870 年 6 月 9 日，狄更斯逝世，舉世哀悼，並同其他英國傑出小說家被葬於西敏寺（Westminster Abbey）內。

故事介紹　p. 5

　　《孤星血淚》因其緊湊的故事結構，被譽為狄更斯最好的小說。內容講述一個出生貧寒的青年匹普，掙脫艱苦困頓的童年崛起的故事。因為強烈渴求社會地位的攀升，他來到城市。某天一位律師出現，告知匹普他繼承了巨大財產，而後他成為一位紳士。

然而，匹普學會將目光放遠，不拘泥於社會地位與金銀財富這些膚淺的價值標準。他發現他的神秘資助人，是曾受他短暫幫助的一名逃犯，而非他所想的那位上年紀、自我中心的哈維辛小姐。

　　他也發現到，他以為出生上流、受哈維辛小姐領養的愛人艾絲黛拉，其實是那名逃犯的女兒。哈維辛還長期教導艾絲黛拉去踐踏男人的心，以彌補自己當年被男人拋棄的傷痛。

　　藉由哈維辛小姐，這位生活充滿憎恨的怨懟女子，與粗魯殘忍的班特立‧莊姆，這位艾絲黛拉之後的丈夫，這兩個負面例子使匹普瞧見，那上流生活的夢幻背後缺席的人性。

　　漫遊多年後，匹普終於返鄉。是逃犯麥格威區與貧困的喬舅舅，使他明白人類的內在價值與紳士的行為準則。體會到曾受他鄙棄的逃犯所釋出的關懷，以及身為村里鐵匠的舅舅對他誠摯的愛，匹普因此瞭解這些價值才是他該追求的遠大理想。

p. 10–11

匹普：我很小的時候，父母就過世了。我和姊姊及姊夫喬住在一起。喬很仁慈，我敬他如父。有一天，有個人對我有興趣，出錢讓我受教育，成為一位合乎體統的英國紳士。我很想知道這個人是誰。

艾絲黛拉：我被哈維辛小姐撫養長大，她在我很小的時候便收養了我。我很美麗，很多男人都想和我在一起。然而，哈維辛小姐教我如何殘酷地對待男人。

哈維辛小姐：我是上了年紀的淑女，我恨天下所有的男人，我無法忍受看到情侶們彼此相愛。

喬：我是村裡的鐵匠，匹普是我的內弟，他年紀很小，我和妻子待他有如兒子一般。

麥格威區：我是囚犯，但我計畫越獄兩次。第一次我遇到匹普，第二次我越獄時到了澳洲，成為一位牧羊農場主人，而變得富裕。

碧蒂：我是村裡的兼職老師，當喬的妻子生病時，我搬去他們家照顧她。

［第一章］ 匹普和艾絲黛拉

p. 12-13 故事開始於我七歲那一年。那時我人正在家附近、埋葬雙親的教堂墓地。

　　我一時間感到害怕得開始哭泣了起來，哭聲迴蕩在墓園裡。

　　「是誰在發出了這種可怕的聲音？」一個低沉的聲音説道。一位長相嚇人的男人向我走來。

　　「不要動，不然我就割斷你的喉嚨。」他説道。他一身骯髒，銬著腳鐐，一定是從這附近的監獄脱逃出來的！

　　他把我抓住，我哭喊著：「請你不要殺我！」

　　「你叫什麼名字？快説！」他命令我。

　　「匹普。」我説道。

　　「你家在哪裡？」他問道。我指向附近的村莊。

　　然後他把我整個人倒抓起來，讓我口袋的東西都掉了出來。我只有一片麵包，他很快地撿麵包，狼吞虎嚥地吃了下去。

p. 14-15 「你的父母在哪裡？」他問道。我指向墓地的墓碑。

　　「他們在那邊的地底下，先生。」我答道。

　　「那你和誰住在一起？」

　　「和我姊姊，鐵匠喬‧格丘瑞的太太。」我答道。

　　「鐵匠，哦？你知道銼刀是什麼嗎？」

　　「是的，我知道。」我説。

　　「那你給我拿一把銼刀和一些食物過來，這樣我就不殺你。」他説。

　　我答應他，於是他便放我走了。在我離開之前，他又説了一次：「你今天晚上給我拿一把銼刀和食物過來。聽好了，不要告訴任何人你看到我，假如你説出去的話，我會找到你，把你宰了。」

我害怕極了，就再次承諾會把東西帶回來，而且不會將這件事說出去。之後，我便逃出了墓地。

　　我心裡想，「我必須把他要的東西帶給他，假如我沒有這樣做，他一定會找到我家，把我殺了。他知道我住在哪裡。」

p. 16–17 我很擔心，偷拿屋內的食物不是那麼容易。我姊姊年紀比我大很多，她常常發脾氣。假如被她抓到的話，我一定會被懲罰。但另一方面，她的先生喬對我很仁慈，他通常會保護我，不讓姊姊傷害我。

　　那天晚上，我想辦法要在口袋裡藏一些麵包。姊夫說：「匹普！你吃太快了，不能把你全部的麵包這麼快就吃光，不小心的話身體會不舒服的。」

　　姊姊看著我說道：「他幹了什麼事？」

　　「他吃太快了，我小時候吃東西也是很快，只不過沒有像你那麼快！」喬說。

　　姊姊抓著我的頭髮，把我從椅子上拉起來。

　　「好了！現在該是你吃藥的時間了！」姊姊給我喝一匙「焦油水」，那是一種令人作噁的黑色濃稠液體。太可怕了，我以最快的速度把它吞下去。

p. 18–19 等喬和姊姊入睡之後，我偷偷潛入廚房，從食物櫃迅速拿了個豬肉餡餅，那是喬的叔叔帕伯丘克為了隔天的聖誕晚餐才給姊姊的。

　　接著，我拿了些白蘭地酒，再從喬的工廠拿了一把銼刀。我跑去墓地，很快地把餡餅、白蘭地和銼刀拿給那個嚇人的男子，然後就又直奔回家了。

隔天，我很擔心，我知道姊姊會發現餡餅和白蘭地不見了。

姊姊準備了晚餐，帕伯丘克叔叔和另一位男士屋伯索先生來和我們一起吃晚餐。這真是美好的一餐，用餐快結束時，我開始在想我今晚或許能逃過一劫。

就在這時，姊姊說道：「我差點兒忘記，帕伯丘克叔叔給了我們一個餡餅。」她起身去拿，但空手而回。

「餡餅不見了！」她以驚訝的語氣說道。

我覺得很有罪惡感，便悚然起身，跑到屋外。我跑到前門，把門打開。我嚇了一跳，有一群士兵和一位警察站在門口。

 p. 20–21 這位警察先生說道：「我們要喬幫我們修理這三個東西。」他拿著三副手銬。「昨晚有兩個囚犯越獄了。」

喬把手銬拿過來，修理好後，所有人都加入尋找兩個囚犯的行列。我們穿越原野森林時，我坐在喬的肩上。我希望我能先看到囚犯。我很怕他會認為是我告訴警察有關他的事。

搜尋了一陣子後，傳來一陣叫喊聲。我們跟隨聲音的來源，看到兩個男人在打架。一個就是我給他食物的囚犯，另一個則臉上有一道長條疤痕。這些士兵很快就抓住他們。

當他們要被帶走時，我昨天遇到的那個人看見了我。我搖搖頭，向他示意我有遵守諾言。他看著我，但沒有怒氣。

他轉身向警察說道：「我在鐵匠家偷了一個豬肉餡餅和一些白蘭地酒。」

喬訝異地說道：「對呀，我們有一個豬肉餡餅不見了。」接著，喬又對這位囚犯說：「不管你犯了什麼錯，你都有權利吃東西。」

說罷，士兵們便把這兩位囚犯帶回牢裡。

p. 22–23 在村中，我即將要上小學，屋伯索先生的姨婆在學校裡教書。她年紀很大，常常在課堂中睡著。她有位孫女叫碧蒂，有時會替祖母代課。

她是個孤兒，雖然外表看起來有點髒髒的，但她對所有的學生都很仁慈。她教我讀書寫字。

一個寒冷的冬夜，我坐在喬旁邊，在一塊石板上寫下：

親愛的喬：希望你一切都好。我希望我不久後便能教你識字了。

喬對我寫的字感到很佩服。

「匹普！你好聰明啊！」他驚呼，對著我微笑。

喬承諾我，等我長大以後，要教我如何成為一位鐵匠。但我不想，我夢想著更好的生活。我希望變有錢，整天都可以唸書。我坐著幻想我想要的生活，沉浸在幸福的想像中，但姊姊進來房間時打斷了我。她說：「我們匹普好幸運啊！希望她不要寵壞他了。」

p. 24–25 帕伯丘克先生和我姊姊一同進來，他說道：「她才不是那種會寵溺別人的人。」

「誰？」喬問道。

「哈維辛小姐。」姊姊不耐煩地回答：「她要匹普去她家裡和一個女孩玩，還要付錢給他。他最好過去，省得在這裡給我惹麻煩。」

喬倒一臉驚訝，「她怎麼會知道匹普？」他問。

「笨蛋！」姊姊說，「她不知道啦！帕伯丘克叔叔是他的鄰居，她問他認不認識什麼男孩的，他就好心地提到了匹普。」

帕伯丘克叔叔看起來一臉得意，很驕傲能認識哈維辛小姐。

「這男孩去哈維辛小姐那裡可以賺錢，他應該要心存感激的。」我姊姊說道。

可是我心裡一點也不感激。哈維辛小姐很有錢，但她是個冷淡苛薄的女人。她住在一間空蕩蕩的大房子裡，從來不出門。我不想浪費時間和她住在她的房子裡，但我別無選擇，只好去了。

p. 26　隔天早上，我姊姊強迫我和帕伯丘克叔叔一起離開。我們慢慢走到哈維辛小姐屋前。我們按了門鈴，有位僕人來開門。

她讓我進去，但對帕伯丘克叔叔說道：「她不想要見你！」

我跟著這位僕人，經過黑暗陰鬱的房子，來到了一扇門前。僕人敲了敲門，對我說：「進去吧！」我進入房間，背後的門便啪嗒一聲關了起來。

房間裡有很多蠟燭，哈維辛小姐坐在椅子上。她穿著一身白衣服，戴著許多珠寶，臉上覆蓋著面紗，她是我看過裝扮得最奇怪的人了。

p. 28–29　「你是誰？」她盤問道。

「我叫匹普，夫人。」我說。

「匹普？」

「是的，夫人！是帕伯丘克先生帶來的男孩。我來這裡玩耍。」我告訴她。

「過來這裡。」她說道。

我害怕極了，但我還是走近了一些。我看到她的手錶，是八點四十分，而牆上的時鐘也指著同樣的時間。

她對我說：「你會害怕一個已經許多年沒有見到陽光的女人嗎？」接著，她把手放在胸口上，「你知道這裡有什麼嗎？」他問我。

「你的心。」我回答。「對，已經碎了。」她大聲喊道。然後她說：「一個叫艾絲黛拉的女孩住在這裡，我要你和她一起玩耍，去叫她吧。」

我到門口，呼喚艾絲黛拉，我等了一會兒又叫了一次。終於，我看見一個小小的人影沿著大廳走過來。她進入房間，走到哈維辛小姐旁。

p. 30-31 「我要看妳和這男孩玩紙牌。」她告訴艾絲黛拉。

「和他？」女孩問道。她美麗的臉帶著輕蔑不悅。「他只是一個普通的小工人呀！」

哈維辛小姐在她耳朵旁小聲說道：「妳可以讓他墜入愛河，然後再讓他心碎。」

艾絲黛拉終於坐了下來，開始發牌。我選好了牌，她看著我的手。

「他的手這麼粗糙，一雙靴子那麼笨重，看起來又蠢又笨拙！」她說。

我以前從來沒有這麼自卑過，我看著我的手和靴子。我的衣服很骯髒，頭髮也都糾結在一起。她覺得我一文不值。

我們繼續玩牌，她贏了。之後，第二局由我發牌，她讓我很緊張，所以我就出錯了。

「你很笨，你什麼都不知道嗎？」她怒氣沖沖地說。

她很刻薄，但我沒有回嘴。

p. 32-33 「你為什麼不為自己辯駁呢？」哈維辛小姐說：「她說了那麼多污辱你的字眼，你覺得她人怎麼樣呢？在我耳邊小聲說。」我起身到她那裡去。

我小聲說道：「我覺得她很驕傲。」

「真的？還有別的嗎？」她問。

「我覺得她很漂亮。」

艾絲黛拉聽到我這樣說時，顯得不太高興。

「還有別的嗎？」哈維辛小姐又再問一次。

「她很無禮。」我答道，「還有我想要回家了。」

艾絲黛拉帶我去前門，讓我出去。當她關門時，我看到她的臉，她不屑地看了我一眼。我覺得很難過，哭了起來。我踢庭院的牆壁來發洩，接著，我看到了一位高高瘦瘦的男孩。

「你怎麼進來的？」他問道。

「艾絲黛拉讓我進來的。」

「起來和我打一架。」他命令我。他脫掉外套，雙手握拳。我很害怕，但是我在他臉上打了兩拳，他倒在地上。

「你贏了。」他很有氣概地說道。我並不覺得有勝利的感覺，因為艾絲黛拉讓我很難過。

p. 34–35

了解故事背景：維多利亞時代的紳士

在維多利亞時代之前的英國，匹普從鐵匠學徒要變成英國紳士是不可能發生的。人的社會階級從出生就已經決定，兒女必須傳承父母親的職業。然而，在維多利亞時代，繼承大量錢財或工作努力的人就可能提升其社會地位。

要成為一位合乎體統的英國紳士，匹普必須要很富有。一旦有了錢，他就必須接受學科的教育，像是歷史或文學等。他也必須學習如何表現得彬彬有禮，包括學習合乎體統的說話、問候、穿著、用餐的方式，以及各種的生活禮儀。這也就是為什麼他去向帕其特先生學習。

紳士公認是上流社會的一部分，被認為是行為舉止優雅的人。當然，不是每一位紳士都學會表現得彬彬有禮，莊姆就是個例子。

[第二章]　命運的改變

p. 36–37 接下來的幾個月，摻雜著痛苦和快樂。我每天都要去哈維辛小姐家和艾絲黛拉玩，她每天都對我很惡劣。但除了她的殘酷這一點之外，我為她著迷，也很想看到她。還有，哈維辛小姐習慣我的存在後，也和我交談漸多。

　　有一天，她叫我幫她推輪椅到隔壁房間，這個房間陰陰暗暗的，佈滿了灰塵，隨處可見蜘蛛網。

　　裡面有一個長桌，桌上是結婚喜酒的菜餚，老鼠啃咬著中間已經腐壞的蛋糕。不過，這房間一點也沒有嚇到我，因為哈維辛小姐本來就是一個古怪的女人。

p. 38–39 有一天，哈維辛小姐問道：「你年紀大一點的時候要做些什麼？」

　　我答道：「我會成為喬的學徒，雖然我並不想。我想要成為一位紳士，整天都可以唸書。」

　　我常偷偷想，「希望哈維辛小姐能幫助我成為紳士。」

　　但她從來沒有這麼做，她只供應我晚餐，讓我和艾絲黛拉玩。

　　她說道：「我要你明天帶喬一起過來。你長大了，該是時候學習你終生職業要做的事了。」

　　隔天，喬和我一起去哈維辛小姐家。

　　「這小男孩要當你的學徒，是嗎？」她問喬。

　　「你不是要和我一起工作嗎，匹普？」

　　我感到很羞愧，尤其是我看到艾絲黛拉在嘲笑我時。

　　哈維辛小姐說：「我要你當格丘瑞的學徒，這裡有一點錢，把這些錢給格丘瑞先生，有一天你就會是一位技術高明的鐵匠。」

接著，我到哈維辛小姐家的日子便結束了，我開始學習當鐵匠。我不快樂，擔心有一天艾絲黛拉會看到我佈滿污垢的臉，又再以不屑的眼神看著我。

p. 40-41 我和喬一起工作，時間飛逝。

一年後，我問喬是否可以去探訪哈維辛小姐。

「這樣好嗎？」他答道：「她也許會覺得你要向她討東西。」

「我從未向她為我做的事情道謝過。我們這幾天不忙，我可以花個半天時間去拜訪艾絲哈維辛小姐嗎？」我問道。

喬笑著說，「她的名字不是艾絲哈維辛喔！」

喬最後同意了，喬的另一個工人奧立克也想要求休假，我姊姊要喬不許准假。她和奧立克常爭吵，她覺得他很懶，但是喬最後還是答應讓他休假了。

我很興奮能再見到艾絲黛拉。我把最得體的衣服洗過穿在身上。我很高興地去哈維辛小姐家，不過我到時卻失望透頂。

「艾絲黛拉在歐洲，她在那裡受教育。」哈維辛小姐告訴我。「而且啊，她現在變得更美麗了，人人都對她讚美有加。」

我離開哈維辛小姐裡，心中充滿沮喪，覺得自己當下真的已經失去艾絲黛拉了。

p. 42-43 我走回家，天色昏暗，霧氣凝重。我聽到了遠處開槍的聲音。在途中我遇到了奧立克。

他說道：「有幾個囚犯又越獄了。」

我記得很久前的一個晚上，我在墓地遇到了一個囚犯。

我快到家時，有位鄰居跑過來，告訴我：「有一個囚犯闖進你家，有人被攻擊了。」

我跑回家，看到有人群圍在院子裡。喬和一位醫生在廚房，我姊姊躺在地上。她的頭和背被攻擊數次，身旁有一些腳鐐。

「這些腳鐐多年前就被剪斷了。」喬說。

這是我的那個囚犯剪斷的腳鐐！但是我知道他沒有攻擊姊姊，這攻擊者一定是在墓地發現這些腳鐐，再把它們帶進屋裡頭。只有奧立克會做這種事，沒有其他人和我姊姊結怨。然而卻沒有證據能證明是他做的。

p. 44–45　我有一種強烈的罪惡感，我覺得我要為此事負責，因為我提供了武器。

姊姊活了下來，但卻變了很多。從某些方面來說，這是好事，因為她不再大呼小叫，也不再耐不住性子。不過她也不再碎碎唸，有時候還會不開心。

碧蒂來與我們同住，幫忙照顧我姊姊。碧蒂很聰明也很善良，只不過沒有艾絲黛拉那般的美貌。我希望能和她墜入愛河，但心裡卻還想著艾絲黛拉。

我的生活一如往常，接下來的四年都和喬一起工作。有一天，有位律師傑格斯先生，稍來一些消息給我們。這消息從此改變了我的一生。

「格丘瑞先生，我的委託人要帶走這位小男孩，撫養他成為一位紳士。當然，我們也會賠償你的損失。」傑格斯先生說。

喬答道：「不必了，假如匹普繼承了財富的話，我會讓他去的。」

我愣在那裡，我的夢想成真了，我真高興！只不過要離開喬讓我有罪惡感，因為他一直都對我很好。

p. 46–47　傑格斯先生繼續說道：「這項禮物有兩個條件：你必須維持原來的名字，且贊助人的名字必須保密。這裡有一些錢，去買一些新衣服，你一星期後會去倫敦和帕其特先生和他兒子赫伯特同住。」

「帕其特家！」我心裡想，「他們是哈維辛小姐的親戚，她一定是我的贊助人。」

「這是我的名片，你到達倫敦時，請到這個地址來。」傑格斯先生說完便離開了。

喬和我立刻進屋告訴我姊姊和碧蒂，好運降臨在我身上了。

喬先跑進去，歡呼著說：「我告訴你們，最奇異的事發生了。上帝保佑我們的匹普，他註定要成為一位紳士。」

這兩位女士詫異地看著我。

「恭喜，匹普！」碧蒂說道。但是在她們眼中帶著一絲悲傷，讓我感到生氣。

我心想：「她們兩個人為什麼就不能為我高興些？」

p. 48–49 那天晚上用餐時，大家一直恭喜我，但這對他們來說似乎是很難以置信的，這讓我覺得很奇怪，我不能理解為何如此。我如此好運，卻有一種前所未有的孤單感。

那天晚上，我想到了艾絲黛拉。

「會不會是哈維辛小姐要我和艾絲黛拉結婚呢？」我心裡想著，感到無比快樂。

隔天，我訂製了質料最好的衣服，這些衣服很貴，我很驕傲地拿著向喬和碧蒂炫耀。

「我要走了，要去和哈維辛小姐道再見。」我向他們說。

我抵達的時候，我向她說道：「我的運氣很好，哈維辛小姐，我很感激。」

「的確，我從傑格斯那裡聽到，聽說你被一位有錢人收養了。」哈維辛小姐說道。

「是的，夫人。」我答道。

「你不知道這個人是誰嗎？」她問我。

「不知道，夫人。」我答道，不想把我覺得她就是我的贊助人這個想法說出來。

「好吧！看來你前途無量了，我希望你很好運，希望你永遠不要把匹普這個名字改掉。」她說，「再見，匹普。」

我在她前面跪下，親吻她的手以表示感激，感謝她為我做的每件事。

p. 50　這一天，我要動身前往倫敦。我很興奮，但也很緊張。我很期待成為一位紳士。我很快地吃完早餐，然後我親吻姊姊和碧蒂，向她們道別。擁抱過喬後，我就出發了。

我走進村子裡搭馬車，假如在喬的破舊房子前搭車的話，我會覺得非常尷尬。一離開村莊，我的淚水從臉頰上滑落了下來。

「再見了，喬！」我想著，「再見了，我最親愛的朋友！」

我想到離開這麼好又仁慈的人時，覺得很恐慌。然而我心裡另一方面也很雀躍，我嶄新的新奇生活就要開始了。

[第三章]　新的開始

p. 54–55　我前往倫敦的旅途很愉快，即使要花五個小時的路途，時間也過得很快。抵達時，時間剛好剛過中午十二點。

馬車司機帶我去傑格斯先生的辦公室。這裡並不如我所期待的靜謐，這棟建築看起來陳舊灰暗。

我進入辦公室詢問職員，「我來這裡見傑格斯先生。」

職員答道：「他現在正在開庭，你是匹普先生嗎？」

「是的，我是。」我說道。

「我們在等待你的到來，傑格斯先生說，你抵達時如果他人剛好不在，就帶你去新家。」職員告訴我。

他說罷，便拿起他的外套和帽子，我們就離開了這棟建築。

p. 56-57 他帶我去一間很舒服的小房子。在信箱內，我看到名字寫著「小帕其特先生」。

「就是這裡了，你可以進去，在客廳等。」他說道。

我爬上階梯，進入屋內。我進入客廳不久後，我聽到有人爬上階梯的聲音。有位年紀比我稍長的年輕男子走進房間，帶了幾袋雜貨來。

他看著我問道：「你是匹普先生嗎？」

「是的，我是。」我答道。「你是赫伯特·帕其特先生嗎？」

我們彼此對望，我覺得他看起來很眼熟。

「我們以前就認識了。」他說：「你是和我打架的男生，在哈維辛小姐家的庭院裡把我打倒在地的人。」

我現在記起來了，說：「對呀，沒錯！」兩人都笑了。

「我聽到了你的好消息。」赫伯特告訴我：「我還記得很清楚我們第一次見面的時候。就像你一樣，我是被請去和艾絲黛拉一起玩耍，但哈維辛小姐不喜歡我。結果證明她比較喜歡你，其實這樣很好，因為她是一個夢魘。」

p. 58-59 「你說的她是指誰？哈維辛小姐嗎？」我有點被搞混地問道。

「不，不！我是指艾絲黛拉。哈維辛小姐教她去痛恨男人。」他說，「你知道哈維辛小姐的故事嗎？」

「我不知道。」我回答。

「晚餐時間我再告訴你。」赫伯特答應我。

剩下的下午時間，我整理了我的新房間。等到晚餐時間，赫伯特果真跟我說了哈維辛小姐的事情。

「哈維辛小姐的父親非常富有，他結過兩次婚，和前妻生了哈維辛小姐，和第二任妻子生了一個兒子。因為那個兒子人品不佳，父親就把大部分的財產都給了哈維辛小姐。」

「哈維辛同父異母的弟弟心生妒恨，於是唆使一位朋友假裝和哈維辛小姐談戀愛，向她求婚，結果她答應了，也張羅好了整個婚禮。誰知，婚禮當天，新郎官沒有現身，只捎了一封信給她，信上說他絕不可能娶她。」

接著，我說：「那一定就是為什麼她的時鐘總是停在八點四十分了。她一定是在這個時間收到信的。」

「是的，沒錯。」赫伯特說道，「她那時候停止了所有的時鐘，也從此不再踏出屋外。」

「那你知道艾絲黛拉為何會和哈維辛小姐同住嗎？」我問他。

「我不知道。」他答道。

p. 60–61 之後，我上床睡覺，在明亮的早晨中醒過來。隔天，赫伯特的父親開始教導我成為一位紳士。他是一位很棒的老師，拿了很多書給我唸。

我讀了冒險和懸疑故事，還有論文、喜劇，甚至是劇本。我們通常一起去買東西，他幫我培養良好的生活品味。他教我如何打扮，如何在舞會中舉止得宜。赫伯特也是一位很棒的老師，他教我餐桌禮儀，是我很好的學習對象。

我不是帕其特先生教導的唯一學生，還有其他兩位學生。一位叫做史達塔普，我們成為了很好的朋友。我覺得他是個很窩心、友善的人，我們常一起去划船。

另一位學生叫做班特立・莊姆，我一點都不喜歡他，史達塔普也不喜歡。他個性卑鄙，自大又懶惰。

p. 62–63 有一天，傑格斯先生邀請我和其他同學一起吃晚餐。

史達塔普、莊姆和我在傑格斯的屋內碰面，傑格斯先生好心地帶我們進去他的用餐室。

傑格斯先生問：「今晚和你一起的這些優秀男人是誰呀，匹普？」

我向他介紹史達塔普和莊姆，我很驚訝，因為傑格斯先生似乎很喜歡莊姆。

我們坐下用晚餐，有個約莫四十歲的婦女為我們上第一道菜。她很安靜，手腳俐落地做著工作。她好像有什麼地方讓我覺得很眼熟，只是我想不起來是什麼。

每次她上菜時，我都會仔細地盯著她看。我想知道為什麼她會讓我覺得面熟。

晚餐終於結束了。晚餐時，傑格斯和莊姆講了很多話。

傑格斯先生說：「莊姆先生，我敬你，你以後一定會很成功。」我和史達塔普都很驚訝，傑格斯先生很精明，卻被莊姆給蒙騙了。不幸的是，傑格斯先生將不是唯一被騙的人。

p.64–65 我在倫敦生活愉快，我學到了很多，花很多時間讓自己進步。有一天，我收到碧蒂寄的一封信，上面寫著：

親愛的匹普先生：

格丘瑞先生交代我寫信給你。他計畫要去倫敦看你，他將會在明天上午九點去找你。

碧蒂

附註：即使你現在已經是一位舉止優雅的紳士了，也請你務必要見格丘瑞先生，他是位仁慈友善的人，而你也是。

雖然喬要來倫敦看我是個好消息，但我並不想見他。我還是很關心他，但他現在已經不再適合出現在我的生活中了。

假如我能夠阻止他來我這裡的話，我就會這樣做。我覺得很有罪惡感，因為我不像碧蒂說得那般仁慈。

隔天早上，我很早就起床整理，準備迎接喬的到來。稍晚的時候，我聽到他到來了，聽到他笨重不靈活的靴子踏在階梯上的聲音。我到前門迎接他，讓他進來。

「喬，很高興見到你。你好嗎？」我問他。

「匹普，你好嗎？」他回答。

p. 66–67 喬把帽子放在地上，把我的手放在他手中好一段時間。有好一會兒，我感覺他不想要放手。

「很高興見到你，喬，給我你的帽子。」我說。喬覺得在這房子裡很尷尬，不想給我他的帽子。他把帽子從地上拿起來，緊緊握在手上。

「你變了好多。」他說，「你已經長大成為一位國家會引以為傲的優秀年輕人了。」

我覺得很不自在。我介紹他給赫伯特先生認識時，赫伯特先生要握他的手，喬退卻了。他不像我所認識的喬。

喬只是點頭示意。

「你想喝茶或咖啡，格丘瑞先生？」赫伯特問。

「謝謝你，先生。」喬渾身不自在地說，「有什麼喝的都可以。」

赫伯特提議，「那我們喝咖啡吧！」

喬不喜歡咖啡，所以他說：「咖啡不是有一點苦嗎？」

「那我們喝茶。」赫伯特親切地說道。我們坐下來享用早餐，赫伯特先生倒茶。我們彼此非常拘謹地聊著天，然後赫伯特便離開去工作了。他離開後，我放鬆多了，喬也是。

p. 68–69 「現在只剩我們兩個了，先生。」喬開始說。

我打斷他的話，「你怎麼會稱呼我『先生』，你對我而言就像父親一樣。」

喬緊張地看著我，又開口說：「既然現在只有我們兩個人，我要告訴你從哈維辛小姐那裡得來的一個消息。」

「從哈維辛小姐那裡嗎？」我驚訝地問。

「沒錯，艾絲黛拉回來了，如果你去看她的話，她會很高興的。」

我覺得滿臉發熱，早知道喬帶給我這個消息的話，我就會對他好一點。

喬站了起來，準備要離開。

「你做得很好，匹普，我為你獻上最高的祝福，希望你在倫敦這裡能鴻圖大展。」

「你現在要去哪裡呢？你要回去吃晚餐了嗎？」我問他。

「匹普，我應該回家了，我們現在過著不同的生活。你現在過著舒適的生活，但這並不適合我。我是鄉下的鐵匠，在倫敦這裡我覺得很不自在。願上帝保佑你，匹普。」

喬把帽子戴上，和我道別後便離開了。

p. 70–71

了解故事背景：維多利亞時代的孤兒

狄更斯寫《孤星血淚》一書時，正是孤兒最多的時代。當時生活艱困，工作情況不穩定，醫學科技也尚未發達。

除此之外，一般家庭人口都很多，通常都會有八個以上的小孩。這些因素造成孤兒數目眾多，在倫敦街頭四處可見。

假如孤兒來自富裕家庭，親戚或遺產會讓他們過生活容易得多。然而，大部分的孤兒都是來自窮苦家庭，所以生活非常困苦。

狄更斯自己在很小時就必須在工廠工作，以撫養弟妹，因為他的父親長年坐牢。

許多孤兒院因此設立來收容、撫養和教育貧苦的孤兒。不幸地，許多管理孤兒院的人並不仁慈，孤兒的生活很辛苦。

狄更斯大部分的故事再再顯示這些時期孤兒的艱苦生活，讀者會同情故事裡的人物，也會將他們的故事烙印在心裡。

[第四章] 一些可怕的消息

p. 72-73 隔天，我搭馬車回家鄉。對於喬的拜訪，我感到很有罪惡感，我並沒有盡責地好好對待他。我知道去拜訪哈維辛小姐時，應該去探望喬，以撫慰他在倫敦不愉快的時光。

但我也知道喬會覺得尷尬，他會擔心他髒黑的老房子對我來說已經不夠好了。所以我決定晚上要在村裡的藍豬客棧過夜。我知道我應該先去拜訪喬，但我卻先去了哈維辛小姐家。

「她收養了艾絲黛拉，而我也確定她是我的贊助人。她想必是很喜歡我，而且要我和艾絲黛拉結婚。」我這樣想。每次我想到艾絲黛拉，心裡就舒服多了。

我到了門口，按了門鈴。我很驚訝，因為是一位新的員工來開門，是奧立克，一定是喬把他解雇了。

p. 74-75 奧立克用不屑的眼神看著我說：
「世界上什麼都可能會改變。」

我不理會他，便進入屋內。

宴會廳裡，哈維辛小姐安靜地坐在椅子上，站在壁爐旁的是一位我從未見過的女子。

「哈維辛小姐，聽說妳想見我，我便儘快趕過來了。」

聽到了我的聲音後，在壁爐旁的女子轉過身來，是艾絲黛拉！她已經長大了，變得非常美麗。我覺得我好像一點也沒有改變，還是一個鄉下男孩似的。

艾絲黛拉看著我，哈維辛小姐問她：「他有任何改變嗎，艾絲黛拉？」

「有，他變了很多。」說完，艾絲黛拉便離開了房間。

哈維辛小姐說：「她舉止優雅又美麗，對不對？」她接下來說的話讓我很訝異，她拉著我的手，把我拉近她。

p. 76–77 她在我耳朵旁輕聲說：「愛她吧！愛她吧！愛她吧！假如她愛你的話，愛她吧！假如她拒絕你的話，愛她吧！假如她傷了你的心的話，還是愛她吧！」

我很驚訝，不知如何回答。

「匹普，我領養她就是讓她被愛的！我扶養她就是讓她被愛的！我要你愛她！愛她！」

哈維辛小姐好像失去理智般。

她指著門，「去她那裡吧，匹普！她去花園了，去和她聊聊，和她一起散步。」她命令我。

我便離開哈維辛小姐，去找艾絲黛拉。她站在花園前，背對著我。我笨拙地開口和她說話。

她走路和說話的方式就像一位優雅的淑女，我在她身邊就像個小男孩，而不是我期盼中像個真正的紳士一般。她對我一點興趣也沒有，我確定她沒有像我看待她那般地看待我。

我們在花園裡又走了一會兒，她才倏地向我說道：「我胸口裡有一顆跳動的心臟，這顆心可以被刺傷或射傷，但它卻感受不到愛、熱情或溫柔。」

她用一種很冷淡的口氣和我說話，聲音寒冷空虛，一如哈維辛小姐的房間一般。但是當我望著她的臉時，有某種東西是我曾在別人身上看過的。我一直在想是在哪裡見過，但是想不起來。

p. 78-79 拜訪過哈維辛小姐家後，我便離開立即返回倫敦。我沒有去看喬，我知道我沒辦法如我所想的那樣和他聊天，因為我滿心都想著艾絲黛拉。哈維辛小姐的話一直繚繞在我的耳邊。

幾個月之後，我收到可怕的消息。我姊姊過世了，所以我回到喬的家，看到那裡擠滿了村莊裡的人，每個人臉上都很悲傷。我看到喬坐在角落的椅子上，他看起來很憂愁，一身黑衣。我到他旁邊，問道：「親愛的喬，你還好嗎？」

他抬頭看我，説：「噢，匹普！看到你真好，我很高興你來了。你還記得她充滿青春活力的時候嗎？」

説罷他就在房裡空蕩陰冷的角落哭泣。

之後，喬、我和其他村民到了墓地，將姊姊埋葬在我父母旁邊，並向她道別。即使這一天很令人悲傷，但小鳥仍在枝頭吟唱，微風也正輕吹，舒緩我們沉重的心。

p. 80-81 在我姊姊的葬禮之後，我回到了倫敦。生活一如往常地繼續，最後，我的二十一歲生日到來了。就如我所期待的，傑格斯先生告訴我，我的年收入將會比現在多出很多，而我也很想知道我的贊助人是誰。

但傑格斯先生沒有告訴我，所以我問道：「我想知道，誰這麼仁慈地給了我這些錢。」

傑格斯先生回答：「當你的贊助人要你知道的時候，你自然會知道的。」

我很疑惑，我非常確定那是哈維辛小姐，但我不懂為什麼她不讓我知道。

雖然傑格斯先生那一天帶來了好消息，但他也帶來了一些壞消息。他告訴我，莊姆正在和艾絲黛拉談戀愛。我非常震驚，於是隔天我去找哈維辛小姐。

p. 82–83　我到的時候還很早，我看見哈維辛小姐坐在壁爐旁，艾絲黛拉坐在凳子上編織衣服。我看著她的時候，她很明顯地表現出心煩。她把編織的衣服丟在一旁，不耐煩地站起來。

她這種舉動惹惱了哈維辛小姐，她喊道：「你在做什麼？你討厭我嗎？」

艾絲黛拉咕噥地答道：「我只是厭煩自己。」

「說實話！我知道你討厭我！」這位上了年紀的女人說。艾絲黛拉沒有回答，這讓哈維辛小姐更加生氣。

「你的心如此冷酷！你的心像石頭般堅硬！」

這讓艾絲黛拉很驚訝，她回答：「什麼？你覺得我冷酷？」

「是的，艾絲黛拉！你是很冷酷。」哈維辛小姐說。

每次我看到她們的時候，她們都很平靜。看到她們爭吵讓我很驚訝。

此時艾絲黛拉答道：「好吧，假如我很冷酷，那也都是你造成的，這都必須歸罪於你。」

哈維辛小姐很不高興，她對我說：「匹普！她太驕傲了，對不對？我不是給了她全部的愛了嗎？」

「那是誰教我要冷酷無情的？」艾絲黛拉怒氣沖沖地說，「這都是你的錯。」

p. 84–85　「但是我沒有教你這樣對我。」這位上了年紀的女人傷心地說，她伸出雙臂，要艾絲黛拉過來她這裡。

「你告訴我愛情是有害的。」艾絲黛拉平靜地說。

這兩個女人過好一會兒沒有再說話，似乎爭執已經落幕了。哈維辛小姐坐在椅子上，看起來很悲傷，艾絲黛拉站在壁爐旁，後來又坐回凳子上繼續編織衣服。

既然她們兩個都平靜下來了，我心裡想這是我問艾絲黛拉有關莊姆的事的最佳時機。

「你為什麼會和莊姆在一起？他自私、懶惰、愚蠢、脾氣又差，你值得和比他更好的人在一起的。」我問她。

　　她回答時沒有看我，「蛾和許多醜陋的昆蟲都會飛向燭火，這難道是燭火的錯嗎？」

　　「不，但你不是非要這麼做不可的。」我說。

　　她停下編織，看著壁爐的火。

　　我坐下，看著她的臉。這是個好機會，我要告訴她我的感覺。「艾絲黛拉，我愛你。自從我第一眼看到妳，我就愛上妳了。」我告訴她，「我知道妳從來不曾愛我，或是想要和我在一起，但是不管怎麼樣，我還是愛妳。」

　　「你的話對我一點意義也沒有，我告訴過你我的心感覺不到愛，我已經警告過你了。」她說得對。

p. 86-87 　「我要和班特立・莊姆在一起，他今晚會來和我們一起用晚餐。」她告訴我。

　　我問她：「是的，但妳愛她嗎？妳要和他結婚嗎？」我很害怕聽到艾絲黛拉的回答。我知道假如她和莊姆結婚的話，她在餘生中都會悔恨不已。

　　「我以前就告訴過你，我是不會愛上誰的，但我會和他結婚。」她說。

　　我感覺我好像碎成千個碎片般地。

　　「艾絲黛拉，請不要和他結婚。」我求她說：「哈維辛小姐告訴妳說，愛情是有害的，那只是因為她的心碎了，她想復仇。妳和莊姆在一起，是不會快樂的。」

　　「不管你喜不喜歡，我都會和他結婚。這和你無關，也和我養母無關。這是我自己的決定，就算錯了，也由我承擔。」艾絲黛拉說。

　　我很生氣，大叫道：「莊姆是個笨蛋，他不值得妳這樣的。」

　　艾絲黛拉拉著我的手，說道：「我們從不了解彼此，但至少

161

我們可以試著當朋友。」我拉著她的手，用嘴唇親吻它。我的眼淚滑落到臉頰，滑落到她美麗柔軟的白皙肌膚上。

[第五章] 我的贊助人

`p. 90-91` 時間飛逝，在我覺察前，我已經二十三歲了。我不再和赫伯特的父親同住，赫伯特和我搬到河岸旁一個叫作「花園庭院」的地方。

過去這幾天，倫敦的天氣令人很不舒服，雨下個不停，讓我只得待在屋內。我覺得很抑鬱，赫伯特在法國處理商務，我真想念他的爽朗。

那天晚上，我在房內讀書時，突然聽到腳步聲。我拿著油燈到走廊，大喊道：「有人在那裡嗎？」

「有的。」有個聲音答道。

「你在找什麼？」我問。

這個聲音說道：「匹普先生。」

「我就是匹普先生。」我答道。

`p. 92-93` 有個男人走上階梯，大約六十歲左右，打扮像是水手。

「你要做什麼？」我問他。

「我要告訴你一些事。」他說。他到我的房間，脫掉外套。他伸出雙手要和我握手，但我不認識他，我擔心他是不是瘋了。

「我等這天已經很久了，請給我一點時間吧。」他說。

他坐下，緊張地環顧四周。

「今晚有誰和你在一起嗎？」他問道。

「不好意思。」我說，「你在這裡是個陌生人，沒有權力問這種問題。」

這男人笑了笑，回答：「你很勇敢，我很高興你變得如此勇敢了。」

就在這時，我認出了這個男人。他就是我多年前在墓地看到的人，他是脫逃的囚犯！我不知道該說些什麼，我把手放在他的手上。

p. 94–95 他又說道：「我一直很感激你那天在墓地時幫助了我。」

我放開他的手。「我不需要你為此而感激我，我只希望你已經改過自新了。」我嚴厲地對他說。

他看起來像受到傷害，所以我親切一點地說道：「你留步喝點東西再走吧，你累壞了，又全身濕透。」

我給他一些可以暖和身體的飲料，然後他跟我說了他的際遇。他再次越獄，逃到了澳洲，搖身一變成為一個牧羊農場主人，而且賺了很多錢。

「我看你的生活也過得很好。」他說，「告訴我你的事吧。」

「是這樣的，我有一位贊助人。」我有些結巴地說。

「是嗎！難道說你的年收入數字是五開頭嗎？」他問我。

我很驚訝，因為我的收入是五百英磅。

「他怎麼會知道呢？」我心裡想。

然後他問我：「你在二十一歲之前，一直有一位監護人，對不對？他的名字是 J 開頭的，是嗎？他的名字是不是傑格斯？」

p. 96–97 我感到震驚，我現在知道真相了。這個人就是我的贊助人，而不是我原本所想的哈維辛小姐，這個囚犯看到了我的震驚。

「是的，匹普！是我讓你成為了一位紳士。在你幫助我之後，我就允諾自己要努力工作，這樣你就能過好日子。」他說。

我後退了幾步，覺得很可怕，這樣的人支付我生活的一切費用。我好失望。

我滿心的期待已經化成灰了。哈維辛小姐不是我的贊助人，我多麼希望哈維辛小姐要我娶艾絲黛拉。這一切原來只是夢一場！

然後，我想到喬。「可憐的喬，我為了一個罪犯拋棄了仁慈善良的喬。」

這人再次握我的手，我感覺心臟在胸膛裡劇烈跳動。「我今晚要找個地方睡覺，我已經在海上待了好幾個月了。」他告訴我。

雖然我不想讓這男人待在我的屋內，但還是讓他在赫伯特房裡睡一覺。

p. 98–99 隔天早上，我們一起吃早餐，他告訴我他叫做艾伯爾・麥格威區。他很快地吃完早餐，然後起身把一個錢包放在桌上，裡面塞滿了錢。

「這是給你的，匹普。」他說道，「我要你每樣東西都買最好的，當一位真正的紳士。」

「不。」我大喊道，「我不要你的錢，這不是我的。我只想要知道警察是不是在找你。我希望你不會待太久，你只是要來拜訪一會兒而已，不是嗎？」

「不，我會永久待在英國。」他說，「我可以改變我的容貌，但如果警察抓到我會將我吊死，所以你要找一個地方讓我住。」

我不知道該怎麼做，所以就讓麥格威區躲在我的房間裡。幾天後，赫伯特從法國回來了，我必須告訴他這事。

麥格威區讓赫伯特拿著聖經，說道：「你發誓你不會告訴任何人你有看到我。」我覺得糟透了。赫伯特一直對我很仁慈，我不想強迫他保守這個秘密。

p. 100–101 那一天稍晚，只剩我和赫伯特時，他說：「他不能待在這裡，他必須離開英國，但沒有你他不會走的。」

赫伯特說得沒錯，如果麥格威區待在英國，我永遠也不會自由。我決定再也不要拿他的任何一毛錢，但是他已經供給我那麼多的東西，我不想讓警察抓到他。

他繼續待在我們的公寓，只有晚上才會出去呼吸新鮮空氣。

不久，管理員警告我，説他看到一名陌生人在我們房子外面。這男子有一條長長的刀疤，穿著破舊的衣服。管理員説他似乎往上望著我們的窗戶的樣子。

　　「他一定是跟著麥格威區來的。」我心想。

　　隔天早上，我問：「你知道有一位臉上有條長刀疤的男人嗎？管理員説有一位臉上帶著刀疤的男人在盯著我們的房子看。」

　　「我知道他是誰，他叫做坎皮森。他以前是個紳士，但也是個小偷。」

p. 102–103 他繼續説道：「我很久以前就和他認識了，後來我們成了同夥。我們一起在賽馬比賽中詐欺錢財，他出主意，我去做。我們最後被抓了，而看起來像紳士的他把罪都推到我身上。他在牢裡關了七年，而我卻關了十四年，我發誓有一天一定要復仇。」

　　我看著麥格威區，可以看到他眼中的憤怒。

　　「最後，我們恰好同一晚逃獄，在原野中相遇，並打了起來。也就是你和我在墓地相遇的時候。」他説。

　　我們之間沉默許久，之後他説：「我聽説你認識哈維辛小姐，對嗎？」

　　「是的。」我回答。

　　「那你一定有興趣知道，坎皮森是哈維辛小姐同父異母弟弟的朋友。他就是那位假裝愛上哈維辛小姐的男人，然後在結婚當天將她拋棄。」麥格威區説道。

　　這些難解的謎團開始拼湊在一起了。

p. 104–105 赫伯特和我必須讓麥格威區遠離坎皮森。一星期後，我們將他搬到另一個靠近河岸的地方。他住在赫伯特的女友家，位於迷爾池畔。

　　麥格威區和我計畫搭汽船離開英國。我不知道幾點讓麥格威區上船最安全，所以我每天晚上都划船經過我們的屋子，等待赫伯特的示意。

有一天，我收到傑格斯先生的訊息，他要我和他一起吃晚餐。我去了，聽到哈維辛小姐捎來的消息。

「她希望你能去拜訪她，她也要你知道，艾絲黛拉和莊姆已經結婚了。」傑格斯先生說。

我非常震驚，自麥格威區來後，我就忘記艾絲黛拉的事了。

我坐在那裡想著艾絲黛拉和莊姆，女管家將晚餐端出來。每次她端菜出來時，我心裡一直在想：「她到底讓我想到誰了？」

然後，我忽然想到她長得很像艾絲黛拉，她會是艾絲黛拉的親生母親嗎？那晚，我再也無法思考別的事。

p. 106–107 隔天早上，我啟程去拜訪哈維辛小姐。我抵達時，屋內凌亂不堪，最糟的是艾絲黛拉已經走了。我看到哈維辛小姐坐在宴會廳，看起來很寂寞。

「是誰啊？」她問道。

「我是匹普。」我回答。

我坐在她身旁，她開口說。「我的心不是石頭做的，假如我勸得動艾絲黛拉，我就會去做。我後悔把她撫養得這麼冷酷，假如可以的話，請你原諒我。」她哀求著。

「我已經原諒妳了。」我說。

「我也對別人造成了傷害，你知道的。」

我問她，「艾絲黛拉是誰的孩子？」

哈維辛小姐搖搖頭。

「是傑格斯先生把她帶來給妳，對不對？」

「沒錯，她兩、三歲時，她的親生母親因謀殺罪而被起訴，傑格斯是她的律師，他完全沒有告訴我她母親的事。」

天色已暗，我該離開了。在庭院時，我轉過身再看這老房子最後一眼，卻見到火舌從宴會廳的窗戶竄出！

我跑進屋內，哈維辛小姐老舊的洋裝已經著火了！火勢繼續蔓延，我拉下桌巾將她包裹起來，她痛苦地哀鳴著。

最後，火勢平息了，我看著我的手也被火燒到，燒傷令人疼痛難耐。醫生來處理哈維辛小姐和我的傷口，不久我便離開了。

p. 108–109

了解故事背景：前往澳洲的船隻

十八世紀，英國的法律規定比今日嚴格許多。人民犯謀殺罪會處以絞刑，甚至連偷竊罪也是如此！人民會因為違反婚約或償還不起債務而入獄。在嚴格的法律規定下，英國監獄變得非常擁擠而肇生問題。

此時，英國在世界各地擁有許多殖民地。其中一個殖民地澳洲，腹地廣大但人跡稀少。英國政府決定用船將囚犯運送到澳洲，這樣兩個問題就可以同時獲得解決。

首先，囚犯離開英國後監獄就可以被清空。再者，這樣澳洲就可獲得所需人力，變成一個有生產力的殖民地。囚犯被運送到澳洲，若工作努力，最後就可以重獲自由。

這也就是匹普的贊助人麥格威區，從可憐的囚犯變成富有的牧羊農場主人的緣由。然而，假如這些早期的囚犯回到英國的話，他們就會被送回牢裡，或是被處以死刑。

［第六章］ 另一個新開始

p. 110–111 大火燒傷了我的左手手臂一直到肩膀，右手的傷則沒有那麼嚴重。赫伯特必須每天為我更換繃帶。

有一天，他在幫我更換繃帶時說道：「不久前的一天，我和麥格威區有個有趣的對話，他說他結過婚，據說他的妻子因為吃醋而殺害了別的女人。」

我聽到這事情覺得很驚訝。

「傑格斯為她的案件辯護，沒有人看到她犯罪，所以她並沒有入獄。」赫伯特又說。

「這是什麼時候的事？」我問他。

「大概是他碰到你的時候。他有個和你年齡相仿的孩子，那時在墓園裡，你讓他想到了他失去的孩子，這也就是為什麼他一直幫助你的原因。」

「赫伯特！我猜艾絲黛拉就是麥格威區失去的孩子。」我喊道，「我要查明真相。」

p. 112–113 隔天，我去見傑格斯先生。

「你帶這孩子去見哈維辛小姐，是不是？我知道她的母親是誰，她就是這裡的管家。」我告訴他。

「你真的知道？」他回答。接著，我告訴他哈維辛小姐和麥格威區的故事。

「沒錯，我要幫助沒有未來的貧苦小孩，世界上有很多這樣的小孩。」他說。

「她的父親進出監獄數次，而她的母親則因謀殺罪被起訴。我要幫助這貧苦的孩子，我給了這個孩子一個家，給了她母親一份工作。我們要保守這個秘密，匹普。」

隔天醒來時，我發燒了。我的手臂紅腫，非常疼痛。

我睡了兩天，赫伯特先生幾個小時就會為我換一次繃帶。我必須趕快好起來，星期三才能和麥格威區一起搭汽船，史達塔普同意為我們划船到汽船那裡。

p. 114–115 星期三到來了。我穿上一件厚重的外套，拿著一個袋子。我們沿著河邊划到米爾池畔，麥格威區在等我們。

他進了船，說道：「謝謝你們為我做的，能重獲自由真令人高興。」

「不久，你就能享受自由了。」我說。

我們沿著河划了很久，等到約一點三十分，我們終於看到了汽船的煙霧。和赫伯特道別，令我很難過。

汽船靠得非常近，當我們要呼喚船長時，另一艘船出現了。有三個男人在這艘船上，其中一位是警察。

「你們船上有脫逃的囚犯艾柏爾·麥格威區，逮捕他！」他大聲叫喊。

這艘船攻擊我們，接著，我看到坎皮森在另一艘船上。麥格威區跳向他，這兩個男人跳進了河裡，在水中扭打，接著兩人都不見了。

一會兒之後，我看到麥格威區游泳逃離，但警察抓住了他。警察把他拉進船裡，用手銬將他銬住。

p. 116–117 麥格威區傷勢嚴重，他斷了一根肋骨，一邊的肺臟也受傷了。而坎皮森死了，他溺死了。

麥格威區被帶回牢裡，我到那裡探望他。他變得很虛弱。他以前對我這麼好，我不能再像我遺棄喬一般地遺棄他。

之後，在開庭審判時，他因謀殺坎皮森而獲罪，警察說坎皮森並不是溺死的。現在，麥格威區的餘生都必須在牢裡度過了。

有天早上，他問我，「匹普，你都是第一個到牢裡的人嗎？」

「是啊。」我告訴他，「我們在一起的時間是如此珍貴，不能浪費。」

「謝謝你對我如此忠誠。」麥格威區痛苦地呻吟，把頭放在枕頭上。

「麥格威區，你可以聽到我說的話嗎？」我問道。他握著我的手。

我說：「我知道你有一個深愛卻失去了的孩子，我認識她，也愛她。她是位美麗優雅的淑女。」

麥格威區拉著我的手，親吻我的手。然後，他的頭靜靜地垂下，斷氣了。那天他過世時，面容看起來很平靜。

p. 118-119 麥格威區過世之後，我身體變得很虛弱。我整個身體都在痛，無法移動。在時，兩個男人來討債，我沒有錢，他們便說道：「那你得跟我們走。」

我小聲說道：「如果可以的話，我會去的。但我可能會死在途中。」我聽不到他們的回答。

接下來幾天，我對所發生的事情一點印象也沒有。我夢到了喬，我覺得我看到他坐在房間的椅子上，真是個奇怪的夢。

有一天，我醒來時，看到喬正在讀我的一本書。

「水！我需要一些水！」我用微弱的聲音說道。有一隻手遞了一杯水給我。

「喬，真的是你嗎？」我問。

「當然，是我啊。」他說。

「喬，我不值得你這樣對我，我對你這麼不好。」

「我們是老朋友，匹普。我會為你做任何事情。」他親切地說。

「你一直都在這裡嗎？」我問道。

「差不多。」他回答：「我們聽說你生病了，所以碧蒂叫我過來。」

「那哈維辛小姐怎麼了？」我問。

「你生病一星期之後，她就過世了。」他說。

p. 120-121 有喬細心的照顧，我很快就復原了。他甚至還帶我去鄉下呼吸新鮮的空氣。有很長時間，我不能走路，但在鄉下我試著走幾步。

我說：「我很快就可以再走路了。」

喬回答：「慢慢來，好嗎？」

幾天之後，喬問我：「你現在覺得好多了嗎？」

「是啊，我覺得每一天都愈來愈好。」我說。

但隔天早上我醒來時，喬離開了。他留下一張字條，說我已經夠健康了，可以再度過著紳士的日子了，他不想造成我的困擾。字條裡面是一張我帳單的收據，他幫我付了全部的錢。

我必須回家向他道謝，而且我也很想念碧蒂。我想要請她嫁給我，我希望她能夠看到我的改變。

三天後，我去探望喬。我去他的工廠，但是關閉了。我從窗戶看進去，到處都是花朵。我走進屋裡，看到喬坐在碧蒂旁邊，兩人穿著最體面的衣服。

碧蒂看到我，大聲喊道：「匹普！今天是我們結婚的日子。」我很高興我沒有告訴喬我要娶碧蒂的計畫。他們兩個看到我都很興奮。

我不能破壞他們的幸福。

p. 122–123 「碧蒂，你有世上最好的丈夫。喬，你有世界上最好的妻子。」我恭喜他們。

接著我說：「我今天要離開英國了，我對你們有所虧欠，我要把你們花在我身上的錢還給你們。我希望你們都過得很好，我也希望你們能有小孩，並請告訴他說我愛你們。我知道，他會比我更好的。」

我離開了他們，進入赫伯特的公司。我努力工作，成為了合夥人。赫伯特最後娶了克雷拉，我們快樂地住在一起。

十一年後，我回去探望喬和碧蒂。我來到他們家，我從窗外看到，碧蒂正在壁爐旁編織衣服，喬抽著菸斗。

我看到一位小男孩坐在廚房椅子上。他們看到我時很高興。

「這是我兒子，匹普。」他們告訴我說，「我們用你的名字為他命名。」

　　我和他們住了幾天，有天晚上，碧蒂問我：「匹普，你為什麼還不結婚啊？」

　　「我想我現在和赫伯特、克雷拉住在一起很開心。」我回答。

　　接著碧蒂又問：「你還常想到她嗎？」

　　碧蒂很了解我的心思，但我只是說：「以前的事都已經過去了。」

　　p. 124–125 我發現艾絲黛拉的婚姻已經畫下句點。她一直不快樂。莊姆常鞭打一匹馬，最終死在馬蹄下。

　　我去拜訪哈維辛小姐的老家，除了庭院牆壁的古老石頭外，其他都變了。大門還是位於原處，我推開大門，在古老的庭院繞了繞，想起我以前常常在這裡。突然，我看到了遠方有個人。

　　「艾絲黛拉！」我喊道。她走了過來，人變了很多。

　　「我變了很多，對吧？」她問。她的美麗帶著溫暖柔和。我們看到長凳，便坐了下來。

　　「很久以前，我們在同樣的地點相遇，很奇妙吧？」我說。

　　「這個老地方讓我難過，我要一樣一樣變賣這裡的東西。你還是住在國外嗎？」她問。

　　「是啊，沒錯。」

　　「你事業很成功吧？」她又問道。

　　「是的，我很努力工作。」我回答。

　　「我常常在想我在你身上失去了什麼，但我現在變得好多了，我了解到生命中什麼東西才是重要的。請告訴我，我沒有失去你的友誼。」她說。

　　「妳在我心中始終佔據了一個特別的位置。」我告訴她。艾絲黛拉笑了，我拉著她的手。我們一起離開這裡，但我們再也不離開彼此了。

Answers

P. 52 **(A)** ❶ T ❷ F ❸ F ❹ T ❺ F

(B) ❶ a ❷ the ❸ the ❹ the ❺ a
❻ The ❼ The ❽ the ❾ the ❿ a ⓫ the

P. 53 **(C)** ❶ b ❷ c

(D) ❶ impressed ❷ clever ❸ imagined
❹ wealthy ❺ disturbed

P. 88 **(A)** ❶ Pip, Miss Havisham ❷ Miss Havisham, Estella
❸ Estella, Pip ❹ Orlick ❺ Pip, Estella ❻ Joe, Pip

(B) ❶ He asked a friend to pretend to fall in love with her.
❷ He taught me how to dress and how to behave at parties.
❸ Dinner was served by a woman who looked about forty years old.

P. 89 **(C)** ❸ → ❺ → ❷ → ❶ → ❹

(D) ❶ returned ❷ had expected ❸ came
❹ didn't tell ❺ gives ❻ replied

P. 126 **(A)** ❶ (e) ❷ (a) ❸ (f) ❹ (d) ❺ (b) ❻ (c)

(B) ❶ The police caught Magwitch as he was waiting to get onto the steamer.
❷ Compeyson was found drowned in the river.
❸ Joe came and took care of Pip until he fully recovered.

P. 127   C   ❶ c   ❷ b

D   ❶ damaged   ❷ drowned   ❸ abandon
     ❹ had abandoned   ❺ guilty   ❻ killing

P. 136   A   ❶ stranger visited   ❷ taking care of
     ❸ was going to   ❹ while he was ❺ were arguing

B   ❶ I don't deserve to be treated so well after I treated you so badly. (Pip)
     ❷ Love her, love her, love her! If she rejects you, love her. (Miss Havisham)
     ❸ You bring me a file and some food and then I won't kill you. (Magwitch)
     ❹ She stopped all of the clocks just then and never went out of the house again. (Herbert)
     ❺ Mr. Drummle. I drink to you. You will be very successful in life. (Mr. Jaggers)

P. 137   C   ❶ What is Estella's relationship to Magwitch? (b)
     ❷ Why did Magwitch decide to help Pip become a gentleman? (b)

D   ❶ Pip realized that he had met Herbert many years ago.
     ❷ Pip took a pork pie and a bottle of brandy from his sister's house.
     ❸ Pip learned how to become a blacksmith from Joe.
     ❹ Pip played cards with Estella at Miss Havisham's house.
     ❺ Pip's sister was attacked when she was at home.
     < ❷ → ❹ → ❸ → ❺ → ❶ >

175

孤星血淚【二版】
Great Expectations

作者 _ 查爾斯・狄更斯
　　　（Charles Dickens）
改寫 _ Louise Benette, David Hwang
插圖 _ Helene Zarubina
翻譯 / 編輯 _ 劉心怡
作者 / 故事簡介翻譯 _ 王采翎
校對 _王采翎
封面設計 _ 林書玉
排版 _ 葳豐
播音員 _ Kathleen Adrian
製程管理 _ 洪巧玲
發行人 _ 周均亮
出版者 _ 寂天文化事業股份有限公司
電話 _ +886-2-2365-9739
傳真 _ +886-2-2365-9835
網址 _ www.icosmos.com.tw
讀者服務 _ onlineservice@icosmos.com.tw
出版日期 _ 2019年9月 二版一刷（250201）
郵撥帳號 _ 1998620-0 寂天文化事業股份有限公司

Adaptors
Louise Benette
Macquarie University (MA, TESOL)
Ewha Womans University, English Chief Instructor, CEO at EDITUS

David Hwang
Michigan State University (MA, TESOL)
Sookmyung Women's University, English Instructor

國家圖書館出版品預行編目資料

孤星血淚 / Charles Dickens 原著；Louise Benette, David Hwang 改編 . -- 二版 . -- [臺北市]：寂天文化，2019.09
　　面；　公分 . -- (Grade 5 經典文學讀本)
譯自：Great expectations
ISBN 978-986-318-842-1 (25K 平裝附光碟片)

1. 英語 2. 讀本

805.18　　　　　　　　　　　108014311